"The moon is so beautiful," Michelle said, looking up.

"Yes, but not as beautiful as you are," I said, planting my hands on her waist. "I want you." I pulled her to me and kissed her, gently at first, and then more insistently.

"I—I want you, too, Clint," she finally said.

She came to me now, her mouth open and eager, and I matched her eagerness with my own. I held her tightly to me, and if there was anyone else on that deck—or even the boat—we forgot about them totally . . .

Don't miss any of the lusty, hard-riding action in the new Charter Western series, THE GUNSMITH:

THE GUNSMITH #1: MACKLIN'S WOMEN
THE GUNSMITH #2: THE CHINESE GUNMEN
THE GUNSMITH #3: THE WOMAN HUNT
THE GUNSMITH #4: THE GUNS OF ABILENE
THE GUNSMITH #5: THREE GUNS FOR GLORY
THE GUNSMITH #6: LEADTOWN
THE GUNSMITH #7: THE LONGHORN WAR
THE GUNSMITH #8: QUANAH'S REVENGE
THE GUNSMITH #9: HEAVYWEIGHT GUN
THE GUNSMITH #10: NEW ORLEANS FIRE
THE GUNSMITH #11: ONE-HANDED GUN
THE GUNSMITH #12: THE CANADIAN PAYROLL
THE GUNSMITH #13: DRAW TO AN INSIDE DEATH
THE GUNSMITH #14: DEAD MAN'S HAND
THE GUNSMITH #15: BANDIT GOLD
THE GUNSMITH #16: BUCKSKINS AND SIX-GUNS
THE GUNSMITH #17: SILVER WAR
THE GUNSMITH #18: HIGH NOON AT LANCASTER
THE GUNSMITH #19: BANDIDO BLOOD
THE GUNSMITH #20: THE DODGE CITY GANG
THE GUNSMITH #21: SASQUATCH HUNT
THE GUNSMITH #22: BULLETS AND BALLOTS
THE GUNSMITH #23: THE RIVERBOAT GANG

NEW ORLEANS FIRE

J.R. ROBERTS

CHARTER BOOKS, NEW YORK

THE GUNSMITH #10: NEW ORLEANS FIRE

A Charter Book / published by arrangement with
the author

PRINTING HISTORY
Charter original / October 1982
Second printing / March 1983
Third printing / December 1983

All rights reserved.
Copyright © 1982 by Robert J. Randisi
This book may not be reproduced in whole or in part,
by mimeograph or any other means, without permission.
For information address: The Berkley Publishing Group,
200 Madison Avenue, New York, N.Y. 10016.

ISBN: 0-441-30924-0

Charter Books are published by The Berkley Publishing Group,
200 Madison Avenue, New York, N.Y. 10016.
PRINTED IN THE UNITED STATES OF AMERICA

To my wife, Anna,
the Fire in my life

THE GUNSMITH #10
NEW ORLEANS FIRE

PROLOGUE
March 4, 1873
Washington, D.C.

It was day one of Ulysses S. Grant's second term as President of the United States. The elation of victory, however, was gone and Grant, fifty-four days shy of his fifty-first birthday, wondered why he would want to put himself through four more years of horseshit and politicians. Maybe he should have retired and gone back to Point Pleasant, Ohio, where he was born, to be a private citizen.

But he had tried that in 1854, when he resigned from the army as a captain, only to come back in 1861 as a brigadier general. No, he didn't suppose that private citizenry was for him. The aggravation was part of what made him feel alive.

Grant was a Methodist of English-Scotch ancestry who had been in his time a farmer, a real-estate agent, a leather-store clerk and a customs-house clerk, but never had he felt as alive as he did when he was a soldier, a politician, and now President.

Grant poured himself a whiskey and lit a cigar, both of which were within easy reach of his desk in his White House office. At that moment, President Grant's secretary entered the office and said, "Mr. Fenton is here for your meeting, sir."

"Yes, yes, send him in," he said gruffly. He cleared his throat and then went into a coughing fit that lasted until Fenton was ushered into the room.

"You should get that checked, sir," Fenton said, respectfully.

"Yes, that's what Julia keeps telling me," the President said. "Sit down, Mr. Fenton, sit down."

Fenton obeyed and sat in front of Grant's desk. Fenton was a dapper man of about forty, tall and slender, sometimes positively delicate looking, which may have been why Grant—a bear of a man, gruff and unkempt at the best of times—was uncomfortable around him. Still, the President had to admit that the man knew how to run the Secret Service.

"What do you have for me, Fenton?" Grant asked.

"We think we've finally got someone who can act as a courier, sir."

"Is that so? One of your men?"

"No, sir. We thought that too risky. There are bound to be factions that will not want this letter delivered."

"I agree, I agree," Grant said. "We all know that the South has never completely accepted defeat."

"That's true enough, sir," Fenton agreed.

"So who is this man, then, if he's not one of yours, eh?" Grant asked.

"He's a friend of one of my men," Fenton answered.

"Is that supposed to be a recommendation?" He's a friend of one of your men? Whose friend is he?"

"James West," Fenton answered.

"A good man," Grant said, "good man, indeed."

"Yes, sir. He's my best."

"I don't suppose he could . . ."

"We don't consider that advisable, sir," Fenton said.

"Oh, we don't, eh?" Grant asked.

"I'm afraid I have something else set up for him, sir," Fenton added.

"I see. Very well, then, who is the man we're entrusting this mission to?"

"His name is Clint Adams."

"Adams?" Grant repeated. "That name sounds familiar."

"He was a lawman for eighteen years before he retired."

"What does he do now?"

"He travels around the country—he was in Abilene with Bill Hickok—"

"That turned out to be a farce, didn't it?"

"None of it was his doing, however," Fenton pointed out quickly.

"I see. You're for this man, I take it."

"Yes, sir."

Grant frowned and said, "The name is still familiar. Maybe a drink will help my memory." He poured himself another whiskey and offered one to Fenton.

"No, thank you, sir."

"Oh, I forgot," Grant said. "You don't drink, do you?"

"No, sir."

"Yes," Grant said, and took a drink. "Adams, Clint Adams."

"Perhaps you'll know him better as the Gunsmith, sir," Fenton said.

"That's it," Grant snapped, jerking his hand and spilling some of his drink, which he barely noticed. "The Gunsmith, of course. The man has quite a reputation with a gun."

"Yes, sir, he does, but beyond that he is a very capable man," Fenton assured Grant.

"I see. Has the man agreed to help us?"

"We believe he will, sir, but I wanted to clear it with you before we approached him."

"It's your department, Mr. Fenton," Grant said around his cigar. "If he's the man you choose, that's fine with me."

"I appreciate the vote of confidence, Mr. President."

"Will he mind . . . being used?" Grant asked.

"I think that's something we'll have to handle when the time comes, Mr. President. Getting the mission completed takes priority at this time."

"I agree wholeheartedly, Mr. Fenton," Grant said. "Go ahead with your plan, then. It has my approval."

"Thank you, sir," Fenton said, rising. "I'll get right on it, sir."

"Oh, Fenton," Grant said as the other man headed for the door.

"Yes, Mr. President?"

"I'd like to meet the Gunsmith sometime," the President said.

"That can probably be arranged, sir," Fenton said, "after the mission."

"Uh-huh," the President said, "if he's alive, you mean."

"Yes, sir," Fenton agreed, "if he's alive."

1

I had been in Washington for the past three days, all expenses paid by the government, and had spent all three nights with a woman named Elvira Moore. We had met in the hotel dining room, dined together, and after that we spent parts of our days and all of our nights together.

Now it was the morning of the fourth day, and I was finally to have my meeting with Daniel Lewis Fenton, the head of Ulysses S. Grant's Secret Service. If it had not been for Jim West who'd asked me to come to Washington for the meeting I would have left two days ago. I don't like to be kept dangling.

And, of course, Elvira had something to do with my staying. She made the waiting much more . . . interesting.

"It looks like my meeting's on for today," I told her as we lay in bed that morning.

"It's finally been set?" she asked.

"Yes," I replied. "This morning."

"I see. That means that you may be gone by tonight."

"It's possible," I admitted.

"Well, then," she said, turning towards me,

"we might as well make the last time the best."

She was a tall, full-bodied brunette of about thirty, very sophisticated. But when she got into bed, all the sophistication melted away before the fires of her passion.

She pressed her large breasts to my face and I flicked out my tongue, playing first with one nipple, and then the other. My hands roamed her body, and then my right hand nestled between her legs, teasing her to readiness. Her mouth was pressed to mine and she climbed aboard me without breaking that contact. I penetrated to her core, where it was so hot I thought I would melt. She began to move her hips and moan into my mouth, and I put my hands on her buttocks so that I could control the tempo.

Her mouth bit mine, her breasts were heavy on my chest, and her hands reached between us to tickle my balls as I slowly increased the tempo of my thrusts. Finally, she began to lose control. She broke the kiss and sat up on me, throwing her head back, surrendering herself fully to sensation. She placed her palms flat on my chest and raised herself up, then brought herself down on me, grinding her hips, forcing me deeper and deeper inside. Her breathing became ragged and labored and finally I knew it was time. As I began to come, I lifted my hips so that we were both raised off the bed. She compressed her lips and flared her nostrils as she continued to grind her hips, milking me for all I could give her, and when she had it, she fell atop me, once again pressing her firm breasts against my chest.

She kissed me lightly on the mouth and said, "Darling." That was all she ever said afterward.

2

The streets in Washington seemed to all have letters on them. K Street, E Street and so on. I caught a carriage outside the hotel and told him to take me to Q Street. Once there, I found the number I had been given and entered.

There was a spinsterish looking woman seated at a desk inside, and I told her who I was.

"Oh, yes, Mr. Adams," she said. "You're expected. Wait just a moment, please." She disappeared down a corridor. Before long she reappeared and said, "Follow me, please."

I followed her down a long hall to a room with massive oak double doors. She opened them and said, "You may go in."

I stepped through and she shut the doors behind her.

The man seated behind the large desk stood up, showing himself to be a rather tall, slim and well-dressed man of forty or so.

"Mr. Adams?" he asked.

"That's right."

"I'm Daniel Lewis Fenton," he said, holding out his hand. He didn't come out from behind the desk, but simply extended his hand over it. I walked up to him and shook it.

"Please," he said. "Sit down."

He took his own suggestion and sat down, so I did likewise.

"Can I offer you a drink?" he asked. "I don't indulge myself, but I have it on hand for those who do."

"No, thank you," I said. "Excuse me, Mr. Fenton, but I didn't come here for a drink. I'd like to find out why the United States Government paid my way to Washington, and then left me sitting in a hotel for three days."

"Did Mr. West tell you anything?" Fenton asked.

"Jim simply asked me to come as a favor to him."

"I see, and that alone was your reason?"

"That was the main reason, yes," I said, "but I'll admit that curiosity entered into it, but even curiosity wasn't enough to keep me entertained for three days."

"Yes, well, we're sorry that you had to wait, but I had to bring this to the President's attention first, and I wasn't able to get an appointment with him till yesterday."

"I see," I said, although I didn't see anything at all . . . yet.

"I can clear up the whole matter to your satisfaction right now."

"Good."

"I only hope you can satisfy us, as well."

"Let's hear your proposition."

"We—er, the United States Government, that is—would like you to deliver a letter for us."

"A letter?"

"Yes, a very important letter."

"That's it?"

"I beg your pardon?"

"That's why you brought me here? Because you want me to deliver a letter?"

"Please, Mr. Adams. This is not just any letter that we're talking about. Please, allow me to explain,"

"Please do."

"The letter must be delivered to a man who lives in New Orleans," he said.

"Why can't one of your men do it?" I asked.

"Please . . . I will explain."

"Sorry," I said. I was getting impatient, but the man seemed to have to go at his own pace.

"It is not just a matter of delivering the letter," he went on. "There are people who do not want this letter delivered. If I sent one of my men, he would be spotted immediately. We need someone who is not connected with the government."

"I see," I said. "Am I to know what the contents of this letter are?"

"We hope you will be satisfied to know that the contents, and the fact that they must be delivered to our man in New Orleans, is vital to the welfare of the nation."

"Mr. Fenton, I like to believe that I'm as patriotic as the next fellow," I said, "but I really don't like working blind. You'll have to tell me something that will really satisfy me."

Fenton frowned. He seemed to disapprove of the quality of my patriotism, but that was his problem. I waited while he made his decision.

"Mr. Adams," he said, speaking even more slowly than before, "the gold reserves in this country are dangerously low. Towards the end of the war, the South is said to have cached a great deal of gold somewhere. I believe that their plan is to dig it up someday and use it to help the South rise up again. We would like to find that gold before that time comes, and by the same token boost our own sagging reserves. That is all I can really tell you."

"This letter tells where the gold is?"

"Not completely. The contents of this letter, together with the knowledge that our man already has, should lead him to the gold."

"Am I to deliver the letter and leave?" I asked. "Is that the total extent of my involvement?"

"Ah, well. We would like you to, ah, stay with our man and . . . help him in any way you can."

"I see," I said. "You don't completely trust him."

"That's not the case at all," he said unconvincingly. "We understand that you were a lawman for many years and are a very capable man. You see, there are factions that would try to stop our man from reaching the gold."

"I see."

"I'm afraid that we, ah, would not be able to offer you any monetary remuneration for this mission."

"You mean you can't pay me," I said.

"Yes, that is what I mean."

"But you would pay all of my expenses?"

"Oh, of course."

"Train tickets, riverboat passage, everything?"

Fenton frowned and said, "Within reason."

I decided to say yes, for several reasons. Patriotism was one, but more importantly, I owed my friend a lot, and he wanted me to go. Another reason was that my life had been without direction the last few months, and here was something to do that had a purpose. The last reason was that I had never been to New Orleans.

"All right, Mr. Fenton, I'll deliver your letter," I said.

His face brightened immediately, and he said, "Excellent! Yes, indeed, excellent." He opened his center desk drawer and took out a large, brown envelope.

"The letter is in here, in a smaller, sealed white envelope," he said. "Also you will find our man's name and address and a complete description. I must ask you to please memorize it, and destroy it."

"Of course," I said, taking the envelope.

"Also there is some, ah, expense money."

"Enough, I hope," I commented.

"Yes, quite." Fenton stood up and I followed. He put out his hand and I took it.

"I will tell the President of your willingness to help, Mr. Adams, be assured."

"Thank you."

"I'm sure he'll want to thank you personally after the mission has been completed."

"I'll look forward to it," I said.

"If you run into any difficulty, please don't hesitate to contact me."

"Oh, I won't, Mr. Fenton," I promised. "You can count on that. At the first sign of serious trouble, you'll be the first to know."

3

I was standing on the deck of the *Mississippi Queen,* leaning over the railing, watching the waters of the muddy Mississippi kiss the bottom of the boat. It was my first time on a riverboat, and aside from some initial queasiness, I was enjoying it very much. The food was good, and the poker was plentiful. I wondered idly how Duke, my big black horse, was enjoying it. It was the first time he'd ever had anything but dirt under his feet, too.

This was the last leg of my trip from Washington to New Orleans. Up until now, most of the traveling had been done by rail, and a little of it by trail.

"Excuse me, sir," a man at my elbow said. I turned and found Henri, a porter, standing at attention.

"Yes, Henri?"

"Dinner, sir. The dining room is now open to serve dinner."

"Thank you, Henri."

I touched my pocket, which bulged comfortably, and decided that I had won enough at poker for one night. I had been taking a break from the game, but with the news that dinner was available, I became aware of the fact that I was hungry.

Henri had been paying special attention to me since I got on board. I wondered if maybe I didn't look like an affluent, riverboat gambler, dressed in my new suit. I tugged at the binding collar of my shirt, and then started for the dining room.

When I entered the dining room I had no trouble choosing where I wanted to sit. There were plenty of empty tables, but none of them appealed to me. The table I wanted was off in a corner, and there was already one person seated at it.

The woman appeared to be in her early twenties. She had very dark hair swept atop her head, and a long, graceful neck. She was wearing a gown cut daringly low in front, showing off full, well-rounded breasts. I had caught a brief look at her as we were boarding and had decided there and then to look for her the first chance I had.

A waiter came to show me to a table, but I waved him off, indicating that I had already picked out the table I wanted. As he started to walk off, though, I called him back and pressed some money into his hand.

"Sir?" he asked.

"In about ten minutes," I told him, "bring a bottle of your best wine to my table."

"Yes, sir," he said. "As you wish."

I walked over towards her table and she did not look up until I was standing right next to her.

"Excuse me," I said.

She looked up at me with large, clear, blue eyes and said, "Yes?"

"May I sit here?"

She gave me a puzzled look, then passed her eyes over the rest of the room.

"There are plenty of tables available," she said, still looking puzzled.

"Yes, but you see, this is my favorite table," I informed her.

"How could that be?" she asked. "This is the first night we are on board. How could this already be your favorite table?"

"That's obvious," I said, sitting down. "It's my favorite because you're sitting here."

She stared at me blankly, then a smile suddenly lit up her eyes and mouth and she said, "That was very good."

"Thank you," I said. "Then you don't mind if I sit here?"

"Oh, but I do," she said, still smiling.

"I'll pay for your dinner," I bargained.

"I'm sorry—" she started to say, but stopped as my waiter approached the table, bearing a bottle of wine.

He showed me the label and asked, "Is this satisfactory, sir?"

I looked at the girl and said, "You see? I need help. I don't know anything about wines."

The girl smiled, then lifted her hand and moved the waiter's hands so that she could see the label.

"That's fine," she said to him.

"Shall I open it?" he asked.

"No," she said.

"Yes," I said at the same time, and since I was the man who had paid him, he proceeded to open it.

"M'sieu—" she began.

"You're French," I said, cutting her off. "My name is Clint Adams, what's yours?"

"Michelle Bouchet," she answered, smiling and frowning at the same time. "Yes, I am of French blood, and you, m'sieu, are very forward."

"Yes," I said, "I am."

"Sir?" the waiter said, extending a small amount of wine to me in a glass.

"The lady will taste it," I said.

"Very good, sir."

He turned and offered the glass to Michelle Bouchet and she took it, tasted the wine, and then nodded. "Excellent."

"You can leave it," I told him. "I'll pour."

"As you wish, sir." He put the bottle down and then asked, "Would you like to order, sir?"

I looked at the lady and she smiled and asked me, "Would you like me to order for you?"

"Have you ordered yet?"

"No."

"Then you can order for both of us."

She nodded, and then spoke to the waiter in French. He understood her perfectly, and replied in the same language, then left, presumably to get our dinner.

"What did you order?" I asked.

"You will see."

"May I call you Michelle?" I asked.

She shook her head in wonder, but said, "Yes, Clint, you may. You are an amazing man."

"You can tell even though we have just met?" I asked.

"I have seen signs," she assured me.

"Well, I'm afraid that incredibly beautiful women bring out the amazing in me," I said.

"I see. Have you known very many?" she asked.

"I've known a lot of beautiful women," I said, peering intently at her, "but none as beautiful as you."

She smiled, then gave me a small frown and said, "Do you know, I believe you are serious."

"I am," I said, and meant it.

Up close, her beauty was overpowering. She had the most delicately shaped, clear blue eyes I had ever seen. Her nose was perfectly shaped for her face, her cheekbones were high and prominent, and her mouth was wide and full-lipped. Her hair was the blackest I'd ever seen, as black as Duke's coat.

Dinner was, very appropriately, fish, deliciously simmered in some kind of sauce that Michelle assured me was very French. She also informed me that the wine was French, as well.

"You don't have a very pronounced French accent," I pointed out.

"Well, as I said, I am of French blood, but my parents always spoke English around me. I can speak fluent French when I have to, but my English is equally fluent."

We finished dinner and sat there talking for hours. Michelle Bouchet turned out to be a remarkably easy woman to talk to.

We finally left the dining room and went out on deck for a walk.

"The moon is so beautiful," she said, looking up.

"Yes," I agreed, "it is, but not as beautiful as you are."

"You keep telling me that," she said.

We were standing at the rail, side by side, and I moved behind her and tried to put my arms around her waist. She started a bit, and slid away, farther down along the rail.

"Michelle—" I began, following.

"Please, Clint—"

"What's wrong?" I asked.

"Nothing."

"Michelle," I said, planting my hands on her waist and turning her around to face me. She was even more beautiful with the moonlight shining on her face. "I want you," I said softly.

I pulled her to me and kissed her, gently at first, and then more insistently. She pulled away and stared at me breathlessly.

"I—I want you, too, Clint," she finally said.

She came to me now, her mouth open and eager, and I matched her eagerness with my own. I held her tightly to me, and, if there was anyone else on that deck—or even on the boat—we forgot about them totally. In the face of what we both felt for each other at that moment, every*one* and every*thing* else just ceased to exist.

Michelle pulled back a few inches and the look on her face seemed to be one of shock.

"Michelle, what is it?" I asked her.

"It's just that," she began, "this is just the last thing I expected when I sat down to dinner."

"What was?"

"That I would end up in some strange man's room."

"I'm not a strange man, am I?" I asked.

She smiled and said, "Not anymore, I suppose."

"And we're not in my room, are we?" I asked.

Now her smile was broader as she said, "No . . . not yet."

4

We walked down to my cabin hand in hand, and I was surprised at how much I truly wanted this woman. My initial concern was to get this lovely woman into my bed, but it had gone beyond that now. If I had stopped to think about it at that moment, it might have scared me.

"Don't talk," she told me as we entered the room. "Please, don't talk."

We undressed each other with controlled eagerness and moved together to the bed. We stared into each other's eyes, and then I made the first move. I touched her proud, full breasts with my fingertips and she closed her eyes and shivered. I stroked her, tweaked her nipples to life, then leaned over and began to run my tongue and lips over her. Her hands came up and cradled my head while I suckled her nipples to hardness. Then she released one hand from my head and sought out my hardness, and stroked it.

I pushed her down on the bed on her back and then lay down next to her. I kissed her and we pressed our bodies together so that our flesh met as our lips did. It seemed as if we were attempting to devour each other as our mouths worked together, our tongues intertwined.

We were content to explore each other's bodies for a long time before I finally rolled her onto her back and straddled her. She spread her legs for me and I eased myself into her slowly. This was one woman I did not want to rush. She stroked my face, neck, shoulders and back as I slid into her, and when I was deep inside, she began running her nails along my shoulders and spine.

I held her buttocks, and then began to take long, easy strokes into her. The pace seemed to suit her as well, for she moved her hips into me easily, and it became the nearest thing to perfect I'd ever had with a woman.

When I felt her building to the brink of her climax I knew we were going to achieve it together. As she shuddered beneath me I let myself empty into her, and I would have sworn that the boat was rocking a little more than normally beneath us.

We were both covered with a fine sheen of perspiration by that time. I slid out of her and began to taste the salt on her breasts. Her hand moved down to manipulate my penis, and I began to respond to her touch. She reached down farther and began to squeeze my sack, then she ran her fingernails along the length of my swollen shaft.

Then she pushed me onto my back, and moved down on the bed to rub my penis against her face. She swiped at it periodically with her tongue, and then suddenly I felt her hot mouth engulf me. She allowed me to slide out of her mouth so she could lick the full length of me, then took me back and began to gently suck. I cradled her head in my hands now, and surrendered myself to her control.

She knew just what she was doing. Several times I felt as if I were going to lose myself into her mouth, but she stopped me each time, and continued to work on me, giving me more pleasure that way than any other woman I'd ever been with.

Finally, she seemed to sense that I'd had enough. She crawled up, raised herself above me and then when she had me positioned right she came down on me, driving my erection deeply into her. It was such a shock that we both cried out. She began to work me in and out of her at an ever increasing rate and once again we found our satisfaction at the same time.

She lay down beside me, and I leaned on one elbow to drink in her beauty, enhanced by our lovemaking.

She pulled me down to her so she could kiss me, a gentle, sweet almost chaste kiss that said more of what she felt than words ever could.

"Thank you," she said.

"Can we talk?" I asked.

"No, please," she said, touching my mouth with her fingertips. "Not now."

"We'll talk in the morning," I said.

"Yes," she said, "in the morning."

She had a pensive look on her face as she drifted off to sleep. In fact, there was another word that came to mind that described her expression more accurately: sad.

5

Apparently, talking to me was something Michelle either didn't want to do, or was afraid to do, for when I awoke in the morning, she was gone.

I dressed quickly and went out to look for her. I checked the dining room first, to see if she was having breakfast, but she wasn't there.

I could have looked over every inch of the *Mississippi Queen,* but there was an easier way to do it.

I found Henri, and asked him.

"Michelle Bouchet?" he repeated when I told him her name.

"That's right."

"The name is not familiar, Mr. Adams."

"She must have a cabin if she was on board, Henri."

"That is true," he agreed. "Why don't you have some breakfast, and I will check the passenger list. And in case she is listed under another name—a married name, perhaps—"

"You'd like a description of the lady?" Henri nodded and I provided him with a detailed report on Mlle. Bouchet's appearance, including what she'd been wearing.

"Let me know as soon as you know anything," I said.

"She must have been quite a lady to have made such an impression on you," he said.

"That's just what she was, Henri," I told him. "A lady."

I went to the dining room and discovered that I was ravenously hungry. I ordered a full breakfast of steak, eggs, and potatoes, with a pot of strong coffee.

I was starting on my second pot of coffee when Henri approached.

"I'm sorry to disappoint you, Mr. Adams," he said, "but there is no passenger on board by the name you have given me."

"Then perhaps she didn't give me her . . . full name," I said.

"Perhaps," said Henri, "only . . ."

"Only what?"

"There are no passengers on board who match the description, either."

The impact of this news was beginning to hit me.

"Are you telling me I imagined an entire evening with a woman?" I said. "Or that I dreamed it?"

"I am not saying that," he said. "I have simply answered your question. I cannot offer an explanation. I'm sorry."

"All right, Henri," I said. "Wait—" I told him, reaching for my wallet.

"That is not necessary, M'sieu. I could not accept."

I could see that he meant it, and I respected his wishes.

"All right, Henri. Thanks anyway."

He left, and I poured myself another cup of coffee. What I really needed was something a lot stronger, though, because either I had imagined an entire night with a beautiful, wonderful woman, or that same woman had just disappeared.

I finished my coffee and, in spite of Henri's report, I searched as much of the *Mississippi Queen* as I could, with no luck.

How could she have gotten off the boat between last night and this morning without anyone noticing? And *why*?

I remembered that, during the short time we'd spent together, I had seen flashes of fear and sadness in between her happiness and passion.

Never had a woman I'd known for such a short time moved me so much. It was difficult for me to think of anything else, even though I knew I had an important delivery to make.

Where could she have gone? Had what we experienced last night frightened her enough to disappear? No, it had to be something more than that. She had been on board, but had not been listed on the passenger manifest. That would indicate that someone on board had helped her.

I wondered who, but that was futile. Anyone who needed some extra money would have been glad to help her. The way she had been dressed last night certainly indicated some degree of affluence. Slipping someone a few extra dollars would not have been a problem for her.

So she had not wanted anyone to know she was on board, and I had ruined that for her by forcing myself on her. Then again, I had only initially forced myself on her. After that it was all by mutual consent. Still, she had been frightened enough to leave the ship, and there was that question again.

How had she gotten off?

6

By the time we docked in New Orleans, I had decided that after delivering the letter, I would do something for myself and go looking for Michelle Bouchet.

I got off the boat first and watched as everyone else left, but did not see anyone even remotely resembling Michelle. I waited until they had unloaded Duke for me and then, reluctantly, left the docks in search of a hotel.

One of the advantages of being in a city as busy and prosperous as New Orleans is the ease with which a hotel with its own livery stable can be found. I surrendered Duke, and the big boy wasn't happy. The ride from the docks was not long enough to suit him, after being cooped up on the boat all this time. I promised him a long ride later on, so he could properly stretch his legs.

I went into the hotel and registered, and they had someone carry my gear up to my room for me.

It was the largest hotel room I'd ever had, except maybe for the one I'd had in Washington. I was glad that expenses were on the U.S. government. I hadn't saved up enough during eighteen years as a lawman to handle this kind of luxury.

The room had a bath of its own, and I made full use of it. I changed my clothes, then sat in a chair by the window to watch the city below.

New Orleans was totally different from anything I'd seen in the West. Most of my life had been spent in and out of western towns. Oh, some of those Texas towns were pretty big, but they were nothing compared with real cities like New Orleans and Washington, D.C.

I closed my eyes and tried to picture the man I was supposed to find: Paul Martel. His physical description had been on that piece of paper I had read and destroyed before I left Washington. While my eyes were closed, however, another image intruded itself into my thoughts: the image of Michelle Bouchet's face.

This isn't going to do, I thought, standing up. I had to keep the two things separate. Logically, the mission for the government should take top priority, especially over a woman I had only just met and known for one night.

However, the way I felt about Michelle Bouchet defied all logic.

I picked up the jacket I had been wearing on the boat and slipped into it. I would wear that jacket almost at all times, because the letter I was to deliver was sewn into the lining.

I headed for the hotel bar, figuring to plot my course of action over a drink or two.

The hotel bar and dining room were one, and the headwaiter asked me which I wished to do, eat or drink.

"I'll just stand at the bar, thanks," I told him.

"As you wish, m'sieu," he said, and allowed me to pass through.

THE GUNSMITH #10: NEW ORLEANS FIRE 31

I walked to the bar and ordered a whiskey. Drink in hand, I turned to survey the room. It was huge, and practically filled, yet the noise level was remarkably low.

"You come in from the West?" the bartender asked.

"That's right," I said, although it wasn't strictly true. "How did you know?"

"Your sidearm," the bartender answered. "Most of these gentlemen who are armed are wearing their weapons underneath their jacket. Many of them are not armed at all."

I looked around and found that he was correct. There wasn't a gun in sight except mine.

"Is that likely to get me in trouble?"

"Not really," he said. "It just immediately labels you as a stranger. You might be questioned by the police once or twice, but that's about it."

"The police," I repeated. In the East—Washington, New Orleans, Boston, Chicago, New York, all the "big" cities—they called their law a "police force." There were no sheriffs or deputies, only police commissioners, police chiefs, and several ranks on down to plain old policeman.

It was odd how east and west of one country could be so totally different. There was no difference when it came to bartenders, however. East or west, they were a talkative bunch, and this one was no different.

"You here for business?" he asked.

"I'm here to see a man," I replied.

"Oh? Who is it? I know a lot of people in New Orleans," he said.

"I bet you do," I said. I debated, then decided that there could be no harm. He might know Martel, at that.

"Paul Martel."

He stared at me for a few moments and I thought I saw a shadow cross his face and cloud his eyes, but then it was gone and he was saying, "Sure, I know Paul Martel."

"If you could give me directions to his address it would be very helpful," I said.

"You could just hail a carriage and give him the address," the bartender said. "He'd take you right there."

"Thanks."

"Except that Martel isn't there," he added. "And neither is the house."

"I don't understand," I said.

"His house was blown up a week ago," he told me. "Dynamited, with him and his wife in it."

"Blown up?"

"Boom," he said, without smiling.

"Wait a minute," I said, putting my empty glass down. "Are you telling me that Martel is dead?"

He filled my glass for me, then said, "Mister, I'm telling you that he's gone."

7

"What's your name?" I asked him.

"George," he said, after a slight hesitation.

"George, let me get this straight," I said, leaning on the bar. "What exactly do you mean by 'gone'?"

"Gone," he said, again. "He left, took off after they blew his house up."

"After who blew his house up?" I asked.

He shrugged and said, "Damned if I know . . . but I'll tell you one thing."

"What?"

"It would have been a damned shame if that wife of his had gotten blown up. Who-ee, but is she a sight!"

"Where did he go?" I asked, ignoring the remark.

"I hear he has a place in the bayou, but I don't know for sure if he's there or not. Anyway, you'd need a guide to lead you to it. There's dangerous swamps in there."

"Are there guides available?"

"You'd have to look around and see if anyone would be willing to take you through."

"I see." I picked up the second drink and drank

it down. When I paid him, he said the second drink was on the house.

"Thanks. How do I get to the police station?"

"Don't bother with directions, friend," he advised me. "Just jump in a buggy and give the driver the address or name of the place you want to go."

"Okay," I said, "thanks again."

"Sure."

I walked out the front entrance of the hotel and found a line of those enclosed buggies they called "cabs." I walked to the first one in line and said, "Do you know where the police station is?"

"Yes, sir."

"Good." I climbed in and shut the door behind me, then stuck my head out and told the driver, "Take me there."

"Yes, sir."

I settled down in the back seat and thought over what the bartender had told me.

Fenton had been right: Someone didn't want Martel to get that letter. But instead of trying to head me off, they had tried to do it at the other end. Luckily, they hadn't killed Martel, but they had driven him into hiding, and made my job a little harder. And now that they had failed with him, maybe they'd come after me after all.

"Police station," the driver called out, jerking the cab to a stop.

I got out, paid the fare, and then looked over the "police station."

It was a substantial building constructed almost entirely of brick, which impressed me; even the most clever criminal would have trouble breaking out of that jail.

In the main hall, a man in a uniform approached me. "Can I help you, sir?"

"Yes, I'd like to talk to someone about the Martel residence."

"The one that was blown up?"

"Yes."

"Excuse me."

He left me standing there and went looking for someone who would want to talk to me.

When he came back he said, "The chief will see you, sir."

"Fine."

He led me to a door that said Chief of Police on it, knocked, and opened it for me.

"You can go in, sir," the uniformed man said.

Inside the chief rose from behind a small desk. He was a short, portly man with full mustache and muttonchops, dressed in a three-piece suit.

"Can I help you?" he asked.

"My name is Clint Adams, sir."

"Sit down, Mr. Adams," he invited. "I'm John Ryder. Tell me how I can help you."

I moved forward and sat in a straight-backed wooden chair that was not designed for comfort.

"You're from out West, aren't you?" he asked.

I was about to ask him how he knew, then remembered my gun.

"Just got into town today," I said.

He laughed.

"We like to think of New Orleans as much more than a town, Mr. Adams."

"I don't blame you," I said.

"Just what is it you came here for?" he asked. "My officer said it had something to do with the bombing of the Martel house."

"Yes. Are you in charge of that investigation?"

"I am. I've taken personal charge of that incident. The Martels are among our most prominent citizens."

"Since I was a lawman for many years out West, chief, I make it a practice to check in with the law enforcement officials of any town—er—city I visit."

"I see. I think that's a wise policy to follow. Why are you interested in the Martels, however?"

"When a friend of mine heard I was coming to New Orleans, he suggested that I look up Paul Martel. Imagine my surprise when, in looking for his house, I was told it had been blown up."

"Yes, we were all rather surprised when that happened," he said.

"Was anyone hurt?" I asked.

"No, luckily the blast was concentrated on a little-used section of the house. The Martels were in another part of the house at the time," the chief explained. "It was a rather large house. Have you been by to see it?"

"No, I haven't."

"Perhaps you should go by there," he said.

"Would you know where Mr. Martel is now?"

His eyebrows shot up and he said, "I don't believe I do—not for sure, anyway. He does have a place in the bayou, but that's dangerous country to travel through unless you have a knowledgeable guide."

"Would you happen to know of such a guide?"

"Are you that eager to meet Paul Martel?" he asked.

"I understand from my friend that he is quite an extraordinary man," I said.

"Yes, yes indeed. And his wife, as well." He

paused for a moment, as if lost in thought. Then he said, "Tell me, Mr. Adams, what hotel are you staying at?"

"The New Orleans House," I said.

"Fine choice. May I see your gun, please?"

I hesitated, because I rarely let anyone handle my gun, but then I handed it over, butt first.

"Interesting," he said, turning it over in his hand. "It looks like a Colt, but it is not."

"It's a basic Colt design, with some of my own modifications," I explained.

"I see that," he said, nodding. "Solid body."

"And it's double action."

He reversed the gun in his hand and held it pointing at one wall, as if he were going to fire it.

"Is it?" he said, looking at it with interest. He then lowered the gun and said, "I'll take your word for it, Mr. Adams."

He picked up a pencil and made a notation on a piece of paper, then reversed the gun in his hand and returned it to me.

"Aren't you the gentleman they call the Gunsmith?" he asked me then, surprising me.

"Yes," I replied. "Yes I am."

"I thought I recognized your name."

"I'm surprised that my reputation has traveled this far," I said.

"Surprised?" he asked. "Not flattered?"

I shook my head. "No," I said. "Just surprised."

He made an "as you wish" gesture with his hands and said, "Nevertheless, your reputation *has* spread this far. We would appreciate it very much if you would do your best to keep your gun in your holster while you're here."

"I hope that this will have been the first and the last time I'll have to remove it," I said.

"There is a way to make sure," he said. He held out his hand. "You could leave it with me."

"No," I said, "I couldn't."

He closed his hand, but left it hanging out there as he said, "Why is that?"

I stood up.

"Well, you've already told me that my reputation has spread this far," I said. "I'm sure you didn't mean my reputation as a tough but fair lawman."

He smiled, withdrew his hand and stood up.

"No, I did not mean that," he admitted. "I was referring to your skill with a gun."

"Obviously," I said. "If I was to be seen walking around without my gun, Chief Ryder, I wouldn't be seen walking around very much longer."

"Oh, I don't think we have anyone here in New Orleans who would be a threat to you with a gun, Mr. Adams."

"Perhaps not, chief," I said, "but there's always somebody willing to give it a try."

He gave me a placating smile and said, "Very well, Mr. Adams. I will rely on your . . . self-control."

"Will you assist me in finding a guide?" I asked.

"I will have someone contact you at your hotel," he said. "Meanwhile, please enjoy all our city has to offer. The ladies of New Orleans are incomparable."

"Yes," I said, thinking of one in particular. "I've already found that out."

8

I caught a cab outside the police station and told him to take me back to my hotel. Halfway there, however, I stuck my head out and gave him the Martel address. He recognized it.

"Ain't nothing left there but a hole in the ground and some splintered wood, friend," he said.

"I like holes in the ground," I told him.

"Have it your way."

"Thanks."

The driver had been exaggerating . . . slightly.

"Wait for me," I told him.

"Sure."

The house had indeed been grand. Even from the ashes I could see that. One corner of it was still standing; presumably that was where the Martels had been when the rest of it blew up. The rest of the house was so thoroughly destroyed, it was almost as though whoever had engineered the blast had intended to leave part of the house untouched.

The front gate and a fence were still intact, and I was about to walk through that gate when I heard my cab start to pull away.

"Hey!" I shouted, turning around. "Where are you going?"

I was sure he heard me, but he kept right on going; I had no hope of catching him on foot.

I was standing there, puzzling about why my driver would have left without having been paid, when I got my answer.

There was one shot, and the bullet tossed up dust within inches of my feet. That solved the problem of what to do next: I had to get out of the line of fire. It also told me why my driver had left me there: He had picked me up in front of the police station specifically to set me up.

Before the second shot was fired, I had drawn my Colt and was already moving towards the only cover available—the house.

A third shot was fired before I finally reached cover. I crouched down by a window available and peered out, trying to figure out where the shots had come from. No doubt one of the selling points of this house for Martel had been its secluded location, but that was of no help to me now. I couldn't even be sure anyone had heard the shots, which was probably what the gunman had been depending on when he made his plans.

I was figuring on one gunman, because the shots sounded like they had come from the same weapon.

I sat with my back to the wall and considered my options. Three walls of the room were still standing, so there was only one way in and one way out.

Except for the window.

The glass had been completely blown out, so there would have been no problem going through it in a hurry. The whole thing would depend on whether or not there really was a single gunman. If there was, and I could get him to commit himself to the blown-out wall of the room as my exit, I could go out the window while he fired in the direction of the missing wall. If, however, there were more than one gunman, one of them would surely have a bead on that window, and as I went through, I could well come out a dead man.

There was an overstuffed couch in the room, which had been damaged, and there was a cushion on it that measured about five feet long. It was the only thing at hand that I could use as a diversion.

Keeping low to the floor, I moved across the room and grabbed the cushion. Once I had it in my hand, and realized how thick it really was, I decided to put it to better use.

I had been planning on throwing it out into the open, hoping it would draw fire, and then diving through the window and getting down the road as fast as my feet could carry me. With it in my hands, however, I decided that it would make a very effective shield, depending on the heaviness of the caliber the gunman was using.

There were some bullets the cushion would stop, and then there were some that it wouldn't.

I was about to find out just what my assailant was using.

I was going to get out through the window, with the cushion, and after getting to my feet I hoped it would shield me long enough to get to a clump of trees that the main road wound around. If I could make it through those trees to the main road, I would be relatively safe. It was a little busier out there, and I might even find a cab to get me away from there, bullet free.

9

I holstered my gun, since I didn't know what to shoot at, and two empty hands made it easier to hold the cushion. I clutched it tightly to my chest, leaving the area below my knees unprotected. I took a deep breath, then stood up, took a running start, and dove through the window.

The gunman fired immediately, rushing it, and he was a couple feet behind me. Before he could correct his error, I was on my feet and running, holding the cushion sideways now. I could feel him holding on me, and then he squeezed off two shots, one of which struck the cushion. The impact jerked my arms a bit, but that only made me run that much faster. He fired about four times between then and the time I made it to the trees, and he struck the cushion once more, a glancing blow.

I could have left the cushion behind, because the man was a terrible shot.

As I reached the edge of the trees I discarded the cushion. I was tempted to alter my plans again, and turn to see if I could pinpoint his location, but decided against it. I knew where I was, and in the moment it would take me to locate him, he could have gotten lucky.

I kept on running, and there were no further shots from behind me. Apparently, he had given up.

As I broke through the trees and onto the main road, there was a cab coming towards me. For a moment, I thought it might be the same one, but it wasn't. I flagged him down and climbed into the back.

"Where to?" he asked.

"New Orleans House," I said, keeping my head inside.

"Where?" he shouted.

"Just move, damn it!" I shouted, and he got us started with a jerk designed to take my head off.

Luckily, that attempt also failed.

10

"Mr. Adams," the hotel clerk said, "did you have a nice evening?"

"It was an adventure," I told him. "Can I get a bottle of whiskey delivered to my room?" I asked.

"Of course, sir," he said. "Ah, one or two glasses?"

The look on his face said that he had received this request many times before.

"Just one," I told him. "I'm drinking alone tonight."

"Ah, but that's not necessary in New Orleans, sir," he said. "If you like, I could make arrangements—"

"Thanks," I told him, "but I like to make my own arrangements. Just one bottle and one glass."

"Yes, sir. Can I do anything else for you?"

"I don't think so."

He looked at me doubtfully and said, "Perhaps you would like to have your suit, ah, cleaned?"

I looked down at myself then and realized how much dirt I had picked up during the last half hour. Instinctively, I felt for the envelope sewn into the lining of the jacket and was relieved to find it still in place.

"Sir?" he asked.

"When the boy brings up the bottle, he can take the suit to be cleaned, but I want it back in the morning."

"As you wish, sir," the clerk said. "Good night."

"Good night."

I went up to my room and undressed. I tore open the lining of the suit and removed the envelope. I realized that my suit could have torn during my acrobatics of that evening, and I could have lost the letter without realizing it. I was going to have to find a safer place to put it until the time came when I could deliver it.

When the boy came up with the whiskey and the glass, I gave him the suit and told him to make sure the ripped lining was repaired as well.

"Of course, sir," he said. I tipped him and he left.

I took the bottle, opened it, and then decided I didn't need the glass after all. I carried the bottle to the window with me and gazed out. At night, the city was beautiful, all lit up as it was, and alive. It reminded me that I was lucky to be alive, as well.

A reasonably well-planned attempt had been made on my life that night. Someone had known that I'd gone to the police station, and had a cab waiting for me outside, to take me to a deserted spot so I could be shot with a minimum of attention. The cabdriver had probably blown it by wanting to get away so quickly. He had warned me by driving off. Had he stayed where he was, I probably would have been shot in the back, and killed.

Which was, I think, probably the only great fear

I had in my life. That it would be taken by someone who I would never even see.

With that sobering thought, I set about to get quietly drunk.

11

The following morning I was in the dining room having breakfast when Chief Ryder came marching in. He glanced around the room and when his eyes settled on me he headed for my table.

"Good morning, Mr. Adams," he greeted.

"Have a seat, chief," I said. "Would you like a cup of coffee?"

"Yes, that would be very nice," he said.

I asked the waiter to bring another cup, and another pot of coffee.

"You drink a lot of coffee?" he asked.

"It helps to get me started in the morning," I said.

"I think that I shall come right to the point this morning, Mr. Adams," the chief said.

"Please do."

"I am given to understand that there was some shooting last night around the Martel house. Would you know anything about that?"

The waiter came with the coffee and the cup and we waited until he walked away to continue.

"Yes, chief, I would know something about it."

He must have expected me to lie about it, because he looked surprised when I admitted it.

"Indeed?"

"Yes."

I went on to explain exactly what had happened, leaving no detail out.

"Did you intend to bring this to my attention?" he asked when I had finished.

"Do you mean, did I intend to make a formal complaint?"

"Yes."

"No, I did not. I did not see the man who was shooting at me at all. I could not give you any kind of a description."

"And the cab driver?"

I shrugged and shook my head as he poured himself a cup of coffee.

"I just climbed into the back of the cab and called out my destination to him," I said. "I couldn't describe him, either."

"Did you fire your gun?" he asked.

"I did not."

"Would you have any objection to my examining your weapon?"

"None at all," I said. I shifted in my seat, as if to draw it out, and asked, "Would you like to do it here and now?"

He smiled and held up one hand.

"It will not be necessary, Mr. Adams," he said. "I believe you."

"Well, good."

"Incidently, I may have found a guide for you," he added.

"Oh? Who?"

"You will see. I asked the guide to come here to your hotel today to speak to you."

"At any particular time?"

He shook his head. "Just sometime today."

"Well, I can't hang around the hotel, but I'm sure we'll connect."

"Going out today?" he asked.

"Is that idle curiosity, or a policeman's curiosity?" I asked him.

"With me, there is no difference," he said.

"I have a telegraph message to send."

"I see."

He finished his coffee very quickly and stood up.

"Thank you for the coffee, Mr. Adams."

"My pleasure," I said. It occurred to me then to ask him another question, and before I could have a second thought, I went ahead and asked him.

"Chief, do you know the name Michelle Bouchet?"

He rubbed his jaw as he thought it over.

"Bouchet, Bouchet," he said, repeating the name. "No, I don't believe I do. Is she a friend of yours?"

"Someone I met on the riverboat," I said.

"Ah, and you would like to meet her again, but you cannot find her. A mystery lady," he said, making it sound very dramatic.

"Yes," I said, simply, because what he said was basically true.

"I am sorry I could not be of more help in your search," he said. "I hope you will be satisfied with your guide."

"I'm sure I will be, chief. Thank you, again."

"We do our best to make a guest of our city happy," he told me, proudly. "Enjoy your day. Oh, and please let me know when you intend to leave."

"Why?" I asked, suspiciously.

"I simply like to keep up on goings as well as comings, Mr. Adams," he explained. "You will let me know, eh?"

"I'll keep you well informed, chief."

"Good," he said, smiling happily.

He turned on his heels and marched out of the dining room, his back straight and his chin held up high. He nodded imperiously to the headwaiter, who executed a small bow as he went by.

Ryder commanded a lot of respect in New Orleans, and he appeared to be good at his job. He must have been, to have known about that shooting last night.

As far as I knew, there had been no one around other than me and whoever had been doing the shooting.

12

Outside the hotel, I chose the third cab in line and told him to take me to a telegraph office. I wanted to send a message to Fenton, though of course I wouldn't be using his real name. I had worded it in my mind the night before and hoped that he would understand it, and that anyone else seeing it would not.

I asked the driver to wait, mainly because I didn't want to have to flag down a passing cab, for fear that the same thing might happen as the night before. At least this one I had picked out at random and could be reasonably sure of.

"How long?" he asked.

"Just long enough for me to send a telegraph message," I said, "then I'll be heading back to the hotel."

He made a show of considering it, and when I handed him a dollar he said, "Okay, I'll wait."

I went into the telegraph office and the clerk gave me a pencil and a piece of paper. I wrote out my message as I had composed it the evening before:

COUSIN HAS MOVED STOP WILL

TRY TO LOCATE AND PASS ON YOUR BEST WISHES STOP WILL LET YOU KNOW WHEN STOP

I made it out to "Uncle" and signed it C.A.

The clerk read it over to make sure he had it right, then I waited while he sent it.

"Do you want to wait for an answer?" he asked.

"That won't be necessary," I said. "If one comes in, though, I'm staying at the New Orleans House."

I half expected my cab to be gone when I came outside, but he was still waiting. I climbed in and told him to take me back to the hotel.

On my return, I decided to look in on poor Duke. He hadn't had a good run since I left Texas and he was starting to feel it.

"Do you want him saddled, sir?" one of the livery clerks asked. There were several clerks there, all ready to saddle a guest's horse at a moment's notice.

"No, I just came by to see how he was doing," I said.

"Of course, sir," the clerk said. "He's a beautiful animal."

"Yes, he is. Thanks."

"Go on in, sir. He's in stall number sixteen, our very best."

"Thank you," I said, hoping it was also the biggest they had. I may not have rated the hotel's "best," but Duke did.

"Hiya, big boy," I said, reaching stall sixteen. He walked over to me and stuck his big head out so I could rub his nose. "How they treating you, huh?"

THE GUNSMITH #10: NEW ORLEANS FIRE 55

"Sir?" I turned and found the same clerk who had admitted me.

"Yes?"

"Is he fast, sir?" the man asked. He appeared to be in his late twenties, tall and lanky, with big, bony hands and a wisp of a mustache.

"Fast?" I asked. "He's like the wind."

"Has he ever raced on a track?" I looked puzzled and he went on, "I'll explain, sir." From his pocket he took out a folded piece of paper and opened it up. It was the size of a wanted poster, and he handed it to me.

It was a poster of sorts, announcing the running of something called the New Orleans Mile.

"A horse race," I said aloud.

"Yes, sir, but they run around in a circle on a track of hard packed dirt."

I nodded, continuing to read. They offered a purse of one thousand dollars to the winning owner. The race was to be run the next day, but entrants were to be accepted up until that very night.

"Very interesting," I said, handing it back.

"Well, sir, you see, there is some betting that goes on before the race," he explained, refolding the paper, "and I'm looking for a horse to put my money on."

"You think I should enter Duke in that race?"

"I would certainly bet on him, sir, and feel fairly secure in doing so."

"How many animals run?" I asked.

"They are anticipating a dozen or so, sir."

"Any of them any good?"

He nodded.

"One horse in particular has won this race for

the past three years, sir," he said. "A golden palomino called Michelle's Dancer."

That coincidence of the horse's name and Duke's need for exercise caused me to decide to enter him in the race. Besides, a thousand dollars was a thousand dollars.

"What's your name?" I asked him.

"Jim, sir," he said, "Jim Beam."

"All right, Jim. I'll tell you what. Can you take care of entering him for me?"

"Of course, sir," he said, eagerly. I gave him the twenty dollar entry fee. "I'll take care of it, sir," he said, and started to rush off.

"Hold on, hold on a minute."

"Sir?"

"If there's going to be some outside action, I'd like a piece of it," I said.

"How much, sir?"

"Well, as much as you can get me. Can you take care of that for me, too?"

"Yes, sir."

"How good is this palomino?" I asked.

"Very good, sir."

"Could we get some kind of odds, since my horse is an unknown factor?"

He smiled broadly and said, "I believe we could, sir."

"See what you can do for me, Jim. I'll make it worth it to you."

"You can trust me, sir," he said.

"Yes, I believe I can," I said. "By the way," I said, as a last thought. "Who owns this horse?"

"Mr. Martel," he said, just before running out, "Mr. Paul Martel."

13

As I went back into the hotel I was thinking that maybe I wouldn't have to go trekking through the bayou after all. If the race was such an event, and Martel's horse had won three years in a row, then he'd most likely show up at the race.

Then my job would be over, and I could look for Michelle, if I still had a mind to. Of course, there was something else to consider. Once Fenton knew that the letter had been delivered—if I decided to end my involvement there, and not play bodyguard to Martel—I would have to start picking up my own expenses.

I still hadn't decided what I wanted to do after actually delivering the letter; a lot would depend on what I thought of Martel, once I'd actually met him.

As I entered the lobby the clerk began to wave at me frantically, calling me over.

"Mr. Adams!" he said, as I approached the desk.

"What's wrong?" I asked.

"There is a . . . a *person* here looking for you," he said, his face plainly showing nothing but distaste for whoever this creature was.

"Where?"

"In the lounge," he said, waving his hand towards the small sitting room between the lobby and the dining room.

"Did he ask for me by name?" I asked.

"*She,* sir. Yes, by name. Please, sir, could you possibly . . ." He seemed to be at a loss for words, so I took him off the hook.

"Don't worry," I said, "if we have business to discuss, we'll do it in my room."

"Thank you, sir," he gushed, looking relieved. Obviously my visitor was not the kind of person the hotel wanted hanging around their lobby in plain view of their guests.

"I'll take care of it," I promised, wondering who in the world it could be. The only woman I knew in Orleans was Michelle Bouchet, and nobody'd mind having her sitting in the lobby, unless they were worried it would look shabby in comparison. I walked over to the lounge, curious as to who would have upset the clerk. I had no trouble spotting the offending person. At first, it looked like someone had piled a bunch of dirty old clothes on one of the sofas, but then the pile of clothes moved as I approached it. I said, "I'm Clint Adams. Are you, er, looking for me?"

"I sure am," she said, and when the pile of clothes stood up I could make out—barely—that beneath the dirt and grime, the "person" *was* a woman.

"Chief Ryder told me you needed a guide through the bayou." she said.

"Yeah, I might. Could we go up to my room and discuss this?" I asked.

She peered at me suspiciously, then said, "Well,

all right. You look like a nice enough fella, and I'm tired of having all these hoity-toity people staring at me."

"This way," I said, and she followed me to the lobby stairs.

I could feel the outraged eyes of the desk clerk on us all the way to the top.

"I don't think that fancy-Dan desk clerk liked me smelling up his hotel," she said as we walked to my room.

I had to agree with the desk clerk there. She did have a distinct odor. I opened the door to my room and let her go in ahead of me, then closed the door behind us.

"Well, Miss . . ."

"Just call me Andy," she said.

"Andy?"

She turned to face me and said, "Yeah, that's right."

"Well, Andy, you have to admit that you don't smell like flowers in the spring."

"Neither do you, but you don't see me complaining, do you?"

"Why do you dress like that?" I asked her.

"Like what?"

"Like . . . that," I said again, pointing.

"Like this?" she asked, looking down at herself. "I guess I just never give much thought to my appearance."

"Well," I said, "if you're going to guide me through the bayou, I think I'll want you to at least take a bath and buy some clean clothes before we start."

"What for?" she asked. "That's the bayou, *mon ami*. Me and the clothes are just going to get dirty again."

"Well, Andy, what makes you qualified to guide me through the bayou?"

"I was born there," she answered. "I lost my Frenchy accent a long time ago, because I been around."

I tried looking past the grime and thought I saw the face of a girl who was about nineteen years old, give or take a year. In fact, without the grime on her face and in her hair, she might not have been bad looking.

"I bet you have."

"Do we have a deal, or what?" she asked.

"How much do you want?"

"You look like an honest man," she said. "Pay me what you think is fair."

"Okay, but the bath and the clothes are part of the deal," I said.

"You buy the clothes?" she asked.

"Yes, I'll pay for the clothes."

"When do you want to leave?"

"Day after tomorrow, if it's still necessary," I told her.

"What do you mean, if it's still necessary?"

"Do you know who I'm looking for?"

"No. The chief just told me you were looking for a guide."

"Paul Martel. Do you know where his place is?"

"Sure, but that's a long trip."

I explained how I was running my horse in the race tomorrow, and if I was able to meet Paul Martel then, the trip through the bayou would no longer be necessary.

"I'll pay you to stand by until then," I added.

"Yeah, sure," she said, seemingly unconcerned

about that. "Listen, have you got an animal who can beat Martel's stallion?"

"I haven't seen his horse," I said, "but I've never seen or heard of anything on four feet who could run faster than my horse."

"Is that so?" she said. "Maybe your horse is worth a bet, then."

"Maybe," I agreed. "I'll see you tomorrow, then?"

"At the race," she said. "You can let me know then if we're still going or not."

As she started for the door I said, "wait a minute, Andy." I counted out some money and gave it to her. "For the clothes, and the bath."

"Oh, yeah," she said, taking it.

"And don't bet it."

She gave me a sheepish look, as if I had read her mind, and then she said, "New clothes, and a bath. The things I do for tall, handsome men."

She left and I went and opened the window to air the room out some. Andy may not have smelled so good, but she seemed fairly sure of herself. I liked that about her, and I was interested in seeing what she would look like when she was cleaned up.

I toyed with the idea of going downstairs to the bar and having a few drinks, but truth be told, I felt kind of out of place down there amid all the New Orleans finery. I wondered if there was a western style saloon around anywhere. I decided to go out and find out.

I went down to the lobby and thought about asking the desk clerk about saloons in the area. He had been very polite to me since my arrival, but I knew that I wasn't much higher in his regard than my new friend, Andy, was. I had been born in the East, but the West was my home, and I knew that it stuck out all over me. I figured the hackies would be a better bet.

Outside, I walked to the last cab in line.

"Where to?" the driver asked.

"Do you know where I can find a saloon that's a little less genteel than the hotel bar?"

He peered at me intently for a few seconds, then asked, "Are you from the West?" I nodded. "Are you looking for a game, too?"

I thought that one over and said, "Why not?"

"Get in, cowboy," he said. "I know just the place for you. It'll be a little bit of home for you."

"What's it called?" I asked.

"The Abilene," he said.

"That sounds like the place," I said, and got in.

"Fine," I said, tossing off the second drink. "Draw me a beer to take with me," I added, throwing the money on the bar.

"Sure."

I took the beer when he offered it and then followed him to the table.

"Boys, this gentleman is looking for a game," he announced to the foursome.

"You found one, mister," one of the men said. "Pull up a chair."

"Do you mind if I have yours?" I asked the man who had spoken. He looked at me hard, to see if I was serious, and I said, "I prefer to sit with my back to the wall."

He looked at his friends, then his face broke into an amused smile and he said, "Our new friend takes the name of this place very seriously." They all laughed together, but he moved, saying, "Sure, friend, sit with your back to the wall."

He had moved one chair over, and I said, "Thanks," and took his vacated chair.

"Deal the cards, Lon," he told one of the other men. "Let's play poker."

As it turned out, they were all displaced westerners who, for one reason or another, were now living in New Orleans. The man who had given me his seat was Deke Mason. The first dealer was Lon Carter. The other two were brothers, Bill and Ben Fletcher. The Fletcher boys were young, in their twenties, and only about a year apart. Mason and Carter were both in their late thirties.

We played without much conversation for the first half hour, fairly low stakes. I won steadily, but it didn't amount to much.

"What say we raise the stakes a little, boys?"

Deke Mason suggested then. "We're not getting anywhere like this."

The others all agreed on cue, but I hesitated noticeably.

"What's the matter, cowboy?" Mason asked. "High stakes scare you a little?" He leaned forward, grinning, and said, "Didn't I hear you telling the bartender that you was in Abilene with Bill Hickok?"

"That's right," I answered.

"Well, then, let's raise the stakes a little."

"Fine," I agreed. "Only I want some of the rules changed.

"Oh, yeah?" he asked. "What rules are those?"

"Well, for one thing, I'd like to be able to win on my own for a while," I said.

"What does that mean?" one of the Fletcher brothers asked.

"I think Mr. Back-against-the-wall is saying that one of us is cheating," Mason said.

"That's not it at all," I replied.

"Then what are you saying?" Mason demanded.

I looked at them all in turn. "I think you're all cheating."

The other three froze as I said that, but Mason laughed and said, "That's an odd complaint from a man who's winning."

"Sure, I'm winning now," I said, "but once the stakes go higher the cards will change. None of you will look like very big winners, but all together you'll win enough to clean me out."

"You're serious," Mason said.

"Dead serious."

"Or maybe just dead," Lon Carter said, looking

at Mason. He was the man they would all follow. If he drew his gun, they'd draw theirs.

"Mason," I said, "if any one of these men so much as touch a gun I'm going to kill you first."

"Is that a fact?" Mason said. "You seem pretty sure of yourself."

"I'm sure enough to know that you won't be around to see the end of it if there's any shooting."

Mason studied my face, then said, "What's your name, friend? I should know the name of a man if I'm gonna kill him."

"Then it won't help you to know mine," I said.

"Well, if that's the case, I'm a doomed man, and I'm entitled to a last request," he said, looking amused by the whole situation. "My last request is to know your name."

I waited long enough for a couple of them to start to get nervous, then said, "Clint Adams."

There was a stunned silence around the table for a few moments. Then Lon Carter said, "Jesus, Deke, he's—

"I know," Mason said, keeping his eyes on me. "I know who he is." He wet his lips with an involuntary flick of his tongue around his mouth, and then said, "The Gunsmith."

"Okay," I told him. "You've had your last request. Now I've got one." Nobody seemed interested enough to ask me what it was, but I told them anyway.

"Stand up and walk out," I said.

They all exchanged glances, and the other three were still waiting for Mason to make their decision for them.

"You know, you men should make your own

decisions about whether you're going to live or die," I told them.

The other three looked at one another again, while Mason continued to stare at me, wishing, I guessed, that he had the guts to go for his gun.

As the others pushed their chairs back, he realized he was about to lose them, so he had to save face. He pushed his chair back roughly and stood up first, saying, "There'll be another time, Mr. Back-against-the-wall Gunsmith. Another time."

"Thanks for the donations," I said, touching my small pile of winnings.

Mason started out of the saloon, backing away, and the other three followed. When they reached the door they turned and almost stumbled over each other getting out.

"What happened?" the bartender asked, coming over to the table. "Why'd they leave?"

"My friend," I told him, "don't be so quick to believe people who say they're from the West."

"They weren't?"

"Oh, they probably were," I said, "but they were using your place to cheat people who thought they were, or who liked to pretend they were."

"They were cheating?" he asked.

"You tell me," I said. "Weren't they *always* sitting here, waiting for a fifth?"

He thought about it and said, "Now that you mention it, yeah, they were. I guess I should thank you.

"I lost you four steady customers."

"If they were cheating, I don't need their money," he said. "But tell me something."

"Sure."

"There were four of them, and one of you. Why did they back down? You didn't even draw your gun."

I collected my money and put it away, then stood up.

"Let me have one last drink and I'll tell you," I said.

"Sure."

We went back to the bar and he set me up another glass of whiskey.

After I tossed it off he said, "All right, how did you do it?"

I smiled at him and started for the door. When I got to it I turned and said, "I told them I was Wild Bill Hickok."

Back at the hotel I went into the dining room and used my small winnings to buy myself dinner. While eating, I wondered if the driver who had brought me to the Abilene was getting a cut of what those four cheated to make. They were small time, because there was no way any of them could make a decent amount of money that way. If their scam had been worth anything, they might have decided to face me and try to save it.

At least the owner had gotten one thing out of the evening. He could always say that Wild Bill Hickok faced down four men one night without drawing his gun, and he'd never be quite sure himself whether he was lying or not.

15

When I came out of the dining room, I found Jim Beam waiting for me in the lobby.

"I got you and your horse entered," he told me, "and I got you plenty of action at three-to-one odds."

"How much action?" I asked.

"About twenty-five hundred dollars worth."

At three-to-one, that meant I stood to collect seventy-five hundred, plus the purse for winning.

"Did you get some?" I asked.

"Sure," he said. "I got enough."

"Do I need anything from you?" I asked.

"No, just be at the track tomorrow morning and they'll give you a number to wear when you ride."

"All right. Where's the track?"

"North, in a field between the city limits and the start of the bayou."

"Okay, Jim, thanks a lot."

"Thank *you*," Jim said. "I stand to make a lot of money for myself when you win tomorrow."

"You've got a lot of faith in me and Duke, don't you?"

"I know horses, Mr. Adams," he said, "and I ain't never seen nothing like that big black of yours."

"We'll do the best we can for you," I promised.

"I'll see you tomorrow, Mr. Adams," Jim said. "I've got to get back and make sure Duke eats right."

He went back, and as I turned to go upstairs, I caught a withering look from the desk clerk. I could just see what he was thinking: Now I was socializing with a common groom.

I winked at him and went up to my room.

I checked on that all important letter, to make sure it was still where I hid it, and once again quelled any urge I might have had to read it. I simply told myself that whatever it said wouldn't mean anything to me, anyway—not without whatever information Paul Martel had in his possession.

I was also interested in finding out what kind of a man Martel was. He was obviously a southerner, but he was willing to help the North find gold that the South had hidden at the end of the war.

No wonder his house had been blown up. If he did show up at the race tomorrow, I was going to have to watch that he didn't get shot right out from under me.

16

Most of the city seemed to have turned out for the New Orleans Mile. The race itself was to be run on a track that was more of an oval than a circle, so that there were two curves and two straightaways. We had to go around the oval twice to complete the mile.

I went to the track early, to see if I could find Paul Martel. I would just have to locate Michelle's Dancer, which would be easy enough.

Jim Beam had met me at Duke's stall, and now I turned to him and said, "Keep him calm, Jim. I'm going to look over the competition."

"There ain't no competition, Mr. Adams," Jim said, running his hand down Duke's nose. "Not for Duke, here."

I was amazed at how Duke tolerated Jim's hands on him. Usually Duke didn't let anyone touch him but me. I put it down to Jim's skill; he really knew how to handle horses.

I walked over to where Michelle's Dancer was standing with an impeccably dressed groom holding his reins.

"He's a beauty," I commented.

"Thank you, sir," the groom said. He appeared

to be about nineteen or twenty, and he held the horse with no affection showing at all. To him it seemed to be just a job.

"Hi, big boy," I said, reaching out to touch the stallion's nose. He shook his head slightly, but when my hand touched him he didn't rear or draw back. He stood for it, and he might have even liked it.

And he was big, there was no doubt about that. He wasn't as big as Duke, but of the other horses there, he was easily the largest.

"How old is he?" I asked.

"Six years old, sir," the groom answered. Just about a year younger than Duke.

"Is the owner here?" I asked. "I'd like to wish him luck."

"Mr. Martel was unable to come, sir," the boy said, "but you can wish me luck if you like." Suddenly a cocky grin creased his face and he didn't look as young as I had first assumed.

"Why is that?" I asked.

"I will be riding the horse."

"Have you ridden him before?"

"Yes, sir," he said, looking cocky again, with a touch of arrogance. "The last three years that he has won this race."

"I see," I said. "Well, I'll do my best to see that you don't win it a fourth time."

"Are you running a horse in the race, sir?" he asked. His artificial politeness was starting to get on my nerves.

"I'm *riding* a horse in the race," I corrected him.

"Oh," he said. "Which one, if I may ask?"

"The big black," I said, pointing. "His name is Duke."

"Duke?" he asked, looking amused. "What a quaint name." He made a show of craning his neck to examine Duke, then looked at me and said, "He looks a bit clumsy, doesn't he?"

I ignored the kid's remark—and him—patted the palomino's neck and said, "Good luck to you, boy."

I felt the groom stiffen, as if he thought I had called him boy, then turned and walked back to Duke.

"Here's your number, Mr. Adams," Jim said, handing me a piece of white cloth with the number one written on it.

"Very appropriate," I said. "Pin it on me, will you, Jim? And do me a favor."

"What's that?" he asked.

"Call me Clint, will you?"

"Sure, Clint." He finished pinning the number to my back and said, "There you go."

When I turned back around he asked, "What did you think of him?"

"Who, the horse or the rider?"

He smiled and said, "Both."

"The horse is an impressive-looking animal," I said. "A real beauty."

"I agree," Jim said. "He's fast and he's got a lot of pride. He wants to win."

"That should make it an interesting race, then," I said, because I knew that Duke liked to run and didn't like to see anybody in front of him.

"What about the rider?"

"He's a little arrogant," I said.

"More than a little," Jim said.

"I thought he was just the horse's groom."

"He was, but then Mr. Martel gave him an opportunity to ride, and he's been a cocky so-and-so ever since."

"I get the feeling that it was more than a betting interest you were looking for when you brought this race to my attention, Jim."

He grinned sheepishly and said, "You got me, Clint. The first time I laid eyes on Duke, I knew that if anyone could wipe that smug look off of Joey Revere's face—"

"That's the rider?"

"Right. I knew that if any horse had a chance to beat Michelle's Dancer, it was Duke."

I put my hand on his shoulder and said, "We'll do our best for you, Jim."

"And for my wallet," he added, and we both laughed.

Then it was time for the riders to bring their horses to the mark. We mounted up and walked our horses up to a length of cord that had been tied across the track. When the cord was dropped, and a shot was fired, that would signal the start.

I had already decided how I would run this race. After all, it was only a mile, and Duke had run longer and farther than that many times. I was going to hold Duke running third or fourth and let someone else's horse go out and set the pace. I was interested to see how that palomino would run.

We lined up according to our numbers. Michelle's Dancer had number four.

I had asked Jim, just before mounting up, how Revere liked to run his horse.

"He's won this race three times," Jim had answered. "Last year he went right to the front and stayed there all the way. The two years before that, he came from behind."

"You can do that with a talented animal," I said.

"You should know," Jim had answered, and wished me luck.

Now Duke and I were lined up behind that rope with the other horses and riders, and I was telling him how good he was, and how he was going to run right over this bunch.

When all twelve of us were in line, the crowd began to get louder, anticipating the start. The rope dropped, the shot went off, and so did we.

Duke broke well, coming away fourth, but that palomino shot out of there like a shot. He ate up the ground in his first three or four strides and he was five lengths ahead of the closest horse. Duke and I were still another three lengths farther back than that.

For about half a mile I didn't worry much. We picked up the horses in front of us fairly easily, and by the half-mile point we were running second, but that golden horse still had a five-length lead, and we couldn't seem to close it up on him.

Duke was running easily, not laboring at all, and from what I could see, Michelle's Dancer was running easily, as well. Still, after three quarters of a mile, we had only closed one length.

That was when I started to worry . . . just a little.

Then, as we were coming out of a turn and straightening out for the finish line, I felt a small hitch in Duke's stride, as if he had realized what he had to do and was making an adjustment. All of a sudden, he was just devouring the ground between us and that front-running streak of gold. I saw Revere's face briefly as he glanced over his shoulder at us, but by the time he realized that we were coming at him, we had gone by him.

Duke won that race going away, beating Michelle's Dancer by five lengths.

Instead of pulling Duke to a sudden stop, I let him continue to run, winding himself down, and when he slowed to a trot, I turned him around and headed on back to the finish line. Joey Revere had already dismounted, and he glowered at me and Duke as we trotted by.

Jim Beam was beaming, jumping up and down and clapping his hands. He had won some money, and he had seen the smile wiped off of Revere's face.

"I've been waiting for this day for three years," he said as we stopped in front of him. "Good boy," he told Duke, patting his neck enthusiastically.

As I dismounted he said, "I was just starting to worry as you were coming around the turn for the last time, and then—I've never seen anything like it! You and Duke were running easy and all of a sudden this big monster is moving like a train. For a minute I thought Revere was stopping, that's how fast you were moving."

"You were worried?" I said to him. "Hell, me and Duke were never worried." Duke swung his head over to look at me and I said, "Were we go."

Duke rolled his eyes at me and looked away. I swear, sometimes I think that animal of mine is part human.

17

I collected the winning purse, and then told Jim to take Duke back to the livery.

"I'll collect our winnings, too," he said, "and meet you in the lobby."

"You meet me up by my room," I told him, and then before he could protest I added, "and if that desk clerk gives you any problem, you tell him I said it was okay."

"Right," he said, grinning. "Where are you going?"

"I've got to locate a few people," I told him. "I'll see you there."

He left, walking Duke back, and I went looking for Joey Revere first.

I found him removing the saddle from Michelle's Dancer.

"He's a good horse, Revere," I said from behind him.

He looked at me over his shoulder and when he saw it was me, he went back to what he was doing.

"You got lucky," I heard him say. "If I had seen you coming sooner you would have never gotten by me."

That rankled me.

"Why can't you just admit you got beat?" I asked him. "As fast as we were moving, you would have never caught us if we went around the track another time."

He turned on me quickly with a sharp remark on the tip of his tongue, but the considerable difference in our size must have made him think better of it.

"I'll tell Mr. Martel you said that," he said, instead.

"I'd like you to tell Mr. Martel something else," I told Revere.

"Oh? What?"

"Tell him I'd like to see him."

He shook his head.

"The boss is staying out of sight, these days."

"After what happened to his house," I said. "I know, but I've come to New Orleans specifically to see him. It's very important. Would you tell him—"

"It doesn't matter what I tell him," he said, cutting me off. "He won't see you or anybody."

I controlled my temper and said, "Just tell him that his uncle sent me. My name is—"

"He doesn't have an Uncle," Revere said, and he turned away from me.

Before I realized what I was doing I had reached out, grabbed him by the shoulder and spun him back around to face me.

"Look, you little weasel," I said. "I've got a message I want delivered to your boss, and you better damn well listen to it, remember it, and deliver it."

He stood before me stiffly, but did not reply. However, neither did he turn away, so I proceeded to give him the entire message.

I repeated the part about my having been sent by his uncle, because that was Fenton's code name.

"My name is Clint Adams, and I have a package for him," I told Revere. "I've got a guide, and I'll be coming through the bayou to see him tomorrow. Have you got that?"

Revere continued to stare at me indignantly, then through clenched teeth he said, "I understand."

"That's all," I said. "Take care of your horse. He's a good animal and deserves better than you."

I turned and walked away from him, and from behind me he threw one last remark.

"Watch out for the swamps."

18

The second person I wanted to find before returning to my hotel was Andy. I wanted to make sure she knew that we were definitely going into the bayou tomorrow.

My mistake, of course, was in looking for the same person I had met yesterday. That person no longer existed, which I found out when the new Andy found me.

"Hey, Mr. Adams," I heard someone call out from behind me. I turned and saw a young girl in boy's clothes advancing on me. It wasn't until she got right up to me that I realized that this was my guide, cleaned up and presentable.

What I saw made me wish I could have seen her in a dress.

She was still a small figure, but she no longer resembled a pile of rags. Her auburn hair was clean, her face was scrubbed, and I was surprised to find a sprinkle of freckles on a face that was very pretty. With the proper care it was easily a face that could become beautiful.

"Andy?" I said.

"Who did you think?" she asked.

"But you're gorgeous," I said, laying it on a little thick. "Why would you want to keep yourself all covered up with dirt?"

"To keep men from looking at me the way you are right now and getting ideas in their heads." She peered at me intently and said, "You ain't getting ideas in your head, are you?"

"Not me," I assured her.

Even in boy's clothes, I could see that she had a trim, firm little figure. But no, I wasn't getting any ideas.

"I won a lot of money on you," she said. "You ran a good race."

"You've got that backwards, Andy," I said. "The horse didn't ride me, I rode the horse."

"You know what I mean," she said, and I nodded to indicate that I did.

"When are we leaving?" she asked.

"Tomorrow morning," I said. "Early. Can you get whatever supplies we'll need?"

"Of course."

"What about my horse? Will I need him?"

She laughed.

"Not in the bayou, my friend. We'll make the trip to Mr. Martel's house on foot and with a little luck we'll be there before nightfall."

"Good," I said. "I think the Chief did me a favor when he sent you to me."

"He did me a favor, too," she said.

"What do you mean?"

"Well, it was either guide you, or go to jail. He caught me, uh, stealing."

"Oh, I see."

"But don't worry, Mr. Adams," she said. "It was a lucky day for both of us. Don't you worry about a thing. I know the bayou like the back of my hand," she assured me.

"All right," I said, "but you've got to start calling me Clint, okay?"

"Whatever you say, Clint. You're the boss. By the way, I'll need some money for supplies," she said.

"How much?" I asked, taking some from my pocket.

"Ten or twelve should do it," she said.

I gave her twenty dollars, and said, "Keep the change."

"Hey, thanks. First light all right with you?"

"Fine."

"See you then," she said, then touched my arm and said, "Great race."

"Thanks."

On the way back to the hotel, I felt a little better about not having to take Duke into the bayou. He'd had some good exercise today, and with a little luck, this Martel and gold matter would be wrapped up in a few days. By then, maybe the idea of looking for Michelle would have worked its way out of my system.

Somehow, though, I doubted that.

I found Jim Beam waiting for me outside my room and invited him in. Once inside, he produced the money we'd won. He had it all in one wad, and peeled off a very small portion of it, which he kept for himself, handing me the rest.

"Do you have enough there?" I asked him.

He waved his hand, and said, "For me, it's plenty. Don't worry, Clint."

"All right. How about a drink?" I asked. "To celebrate."

"Sure."

I took the bottle, poured some into a glass for

him, and then he touched his glass to my bottle and we both drank.

"That's a hell of a horse, Clint," he said. "I knew it when I first saw him, and he proved it today."

"He sure did," I agreed. "He even surprised me a little, Jim, to tell you the truth. As we came out of that turn there was a little hitch in his stride, and suddenly he just took off."

"That was something to see, all right."

"To see?" I said. "It was something to ride, I want to tell you."

We drank again, and then the whiskey was gone.

"I could use another bottle," I said.

"I'll send one up," Jim said, putting the glass down and moving towards the door. "I've got to go, anyway."

"I appreciate it," I said. "And, Jim, thanks again for filling me in about the race."

"You don't have to thank me," he said. "We both made out pretty good on it. I'll send that bottle right up," he said, and I thought I detected a gleam in his eye.

"I'll be heading into the bayou in the morning," I told him, "to find Paul Martel. You take good care of Duke while I'm gone."

"You know I will," he said, and he was right. I knew he'd care for the big horse almost as well as I would. "Be careful in there. I hope you've got a good guide."

"Yeah," I said. "I hope so, too."

He left, and I sat down to await the bottle he was sending up. I just wanted a couple of more drinks before I settled down for the night. I intended to sleep well and be rested and wide awake for my trip.

I was checking on the letter once again when there was a knock on the door. I rehid the letter and then went to open the door for my bottle.

There was a little more than a bottle on the other side.

"Hi," the girl said. She was barely five feet tall, but she had large, rounded breasts and she was showing a lot of them in a low-cut red dress. Her face was wide-eyed and innocently lovely, but I had a feeling that she wasn't innocent at all. In her left hand was my bottle of whiskey.

I had a feeling that my good friend Jim Beam had sent me considerably more than just a bottle.

"I've got your bottle," she said, holding it out in front of her. "Do you want me to leave it with you, or bring it in?"

"Bring it in, please," I said. "You've come all the way up here with it; it wouldn't be gentlemanly of me to send you away without at least one drink."

"Thanks," she said, walking in past me. I closed the door and turned to face her. That dress had probably been held on by a hair, because she hadn't been in the room one full second and she had already shed it.

"I guess you know I didn't just come up here to bring you a bottle," she said, smiling mischievously.

"I guessed," I said, after clearing my throat.

She was very impressive. Those breasts were everything the little red dress promised. Her nipples were very brown and already starting to stand up with anticipation.

"You don't have to pay for this, you know," she said, walking to me and taking my hand. "It's been taken care of." She took my hand and placed my palm on one of her breasts. The nipple felt very hard against my skin. "You can just concentrate on doing what you want to do, and enjoying it."

I was beyond the point of saying no, because her other hand was appreciating just how ready I was.

"Let me help you with these," she said, undoing my pants.

She not only helped me with my pants, but with every other stitch of clothing I was wearing, then she proceeded to help herself.

She got down on her knees and took me in her mouth. She was moaning and cooing all along, like a girl who really enjoyed her job. After a while, I wanted to give her something in return. I reached down and drew her to her feet, then lifted her up and carried her to the bed. She had a marvelously full, firm body, and I intended to investigate it thoroughly.

I started with her nipples, filling my mouth with them and as much of her breasts as I could. Meanwhile, I rubbed my hand over her belly, tangled my fingers in her little thatch of coarse hair, and then dipped my fingers into her. She raised her hips off the bed and pushed against my hand, crying, "Oh, yes, mister. Do that, do that some more . . . *please!*"

I began to do to her what she had done to me, but she didn't take it as well as she dished it out.

"Oh, don't make me wait anymore, mister," she pleaded. "Put it in, put it in me!"

I raised myself over and did what she'd asked me to, sinking slowly into her warmth.

"Yes," she said, sliding her hands over me and resting them on my buttocks. She grasped me there, digging her nails in just slightly, saying, "Oh, *yes!*"

She began to buck beneath me, with a lot of strength for such a little girl. Her legs were surprisingly powerful, and she used them in various ways. First she encircled my waist with them, clamping down and holding me tightly between them, then she released and placed her feet flat on the mattress and proceeded to lift us both off the bed.

"Do it, do it, let it all go!," she moaned, rocking her head from side to side. I could feel her begin to climax, her tight muscles contracting and drawing me ever deeper.

I let it all go then, and when I thought I was done she began to move her hips again, pulling even more from me. At last, we were both spent, and I withdrew and lay down next to her.

"How about that drink now?" she asked.

"Sure," I said.

I got up and walked naked to where she had left the bottle. I started to reach for the glass and she said, "No glass. We'll share the bottle."

"Fine with me," I said, taking the bottle back to the bed and opening it there. I gave it to her first and she took a very healthy drink. I watched her throat ripple as the liquor made its way down, and then she took the bottle from her mouth and said, "Ahhh!"

She passed it to me and I took a healthy drink. She ran one finger over my chest, then continued on down, past my belly to my half-erect penis. She encircled it, taking it into her delicate hand and working it towards total erection again.

"I can tell," she said, concentrating on what she was doing, "that this is going to be a very interesting night."

Yeah, I thought, as she buried her face now between my legs and began to use her tongue, it was supposed to be a night of rest.

What the hell, I thought then. At the very least it would keep me from thinking about Michelle Bouchet.

19

"You look terrible!" Andy told me the following morning.

I knew I looked bad, and I knew that I felt almost as bad as I looked, but I didn't want her to know that.

"I didn't sleep very well," I said.

"Uh-huh," was all she said to that. "You're still gonna have to carry a lot of these supplies, you know."

"I'll carry my share," I assured her. Then I looked at her and said, "I thought you said yesterday that I was the boss."

"That was yesterday," she answered. "I'm the guide, that means you've got to follow me and do what I say. Especially once we get in there," she said, pointing north, towards the bayou. "You take a wrong step, you could end up ass-deep in swamp, and sinking."

"I'll step where you step," I said.

"Good. Let's divvy this stuff up."

I carried my rifle, canteen and most of the food that she had bought. She carried a canteen, and a gunny sack she said held bayou necessities.

"Like what?"

"Like medicines for snake bites, and such. You ever been bit by a rattler?"

"Once," I said. It had been when I had first come West, as a young man. Luckily, I was with someone who knew exactly what to do, and did it fast.

"You remember what it felt like?" she asked.

"I sure do."

"Well, you get bit by one of our bayou swamp vipers, and you're gonna think that rattler was a picnic."

"I'll remember."

"You any good with that gun?" she asked.

"I usually hit what I aim at."

"Okay, but don't shoot unless I say so."

"You're the boss—while we're in the bayou, that is."

"That's fine by me."

"Do you have a gun?"

She showed me a small derringer that she had tucked in her belt. "And I usually hit what I aim at, too."

She picked up her share of the burden and asked, "Are you ready?"

She started off at a brisk pace, and I followed.

She was dressed in the same clothes she had been wearing yesterday, which meant they were still fairly clean. Her natural scent was fresh and sweet. If we were going to be traveling on foot, however, through swamps and the like, the time wasn't too far off when neither one of us would smell like a bunch of flowers. I just hoped, knowing better, that a little dirt and sweat was all we'd have to contend with; I didn't like the idea of getting Andy mixed up in anything else.

20

The bayou was totally alien to me. It seemed to be all trees and water, but trees and water the likes of which I had never seen before. Horses would have been totally useless in there. At one point, we even had to take to a flat raft that Andy told me was left there for anyone who needed to use it. When we got off of it she gave it a slight push, assuring me that it would drift back to the other side to be used by the next traveler.

"How do we get back?"

"There's another way," she assured me, but did not elaborate.

We had traveled halfway when she announced that it was time to take a rest. I had to admit I was glad for the chance to take a breather.

"You want some coffee?" she asked.

"Sure," I answered.

"Unload it, then," she said. "You got it on your back."

While we were having a cup of coffee she said, "It's a lot different when you don't have a horse doing your walking for you, isn't it?"

"I don't mind walking," I told her, "but walking

through this stuff . . ." I finished by shaking my head.

I had walked through deserts and over mountains in my time, but nothing I'd ever encountered had been as tiring as walking through the bayou, lifting your feet over roots, pulling them out of oozing mud with every other step.

"You know we're being followed?" she asked.

In fact, I'd had a feeling that someone might be behind us, but the bayou was so disorienting that my usual instincts were dulled. I was beginning to appreciate Andy's gifts more than ever, since mine were hampered by this bizarre environment.

I did not look around, but stared into my coffee cup as I said, "I had a feeling, but didn't think it was very likely. Not in here."

"Well, it's not only likely," she said. "There's more than one or two, and if you know what to listen for, they're making a hell of a racket."

I dumped the remnants of my coffee onto the ground and put the cup away. "Can we lose them?" I asked.

She thought it over. "Maybe. I'd have to travel faster than I'd like to in the bayou. That's not always the safest thing to do."

She looked over at my rifle, then grabbed it and said, "Why don't we wait for them to catch up and take care of them?"

I grabbed the rifle from her quickly and said, "If there's any shooting to be done, it won't have to be done with a rifle. I don't go in for ambushing people."

"So what *do* you go in for? Letting them follow us to Martel's house?"

The question in my mind was, were they after

me for some reason, or were these the same people who had blown up Martel's house, hoping that now I would lead them to him so they could finish the job?

"No, we can't do that, either."

She finished her coffee, dumped the remains and handed me the cup to put away.

"Okay," she said. "I guess we'll have to lose them, but be careful. Step where I step. I'm trying to lose *them,* not *you.*"

"You lead and I'll follow, Andy," I said.

We continued on at a considerably stepped-up pace, and if our pursuers did not have someone with them who knew the bayou as well as Andy did, they were likely to find themselves, as Andy had put it before, ass deep in a swamp.

For a small girl, she sure could move fast. I had much longer legs, and it was a chore for me to keep pace with her.

After we'd gone a few miles, I asked whether she thought we'd lost them yet.

"Stop," she said. .

We stood still, Andy listening intently.

"I can still hear them, but they're farther back now. A few more brisk miles should do it."

"Great."

I took one step forward and suddenly sank in mud up to my knee.

"Shit," I snapped. She heard me and turned around quick to see what was on my mind.

"Step where I step."

I pulled my leg out, the mud letting me go reluctantly with a wet smack.

"Yeah, yeah," I said, kicking my leg to get rid of most of the mud.

After another few miles she stopped me again and listened, then nodded. "Okay," she said. "I can hardly hear them anymore."

"Won't they just have to keep going in this direction to get there?" I asked.

"Sure," she said. "I hope they do keep going straight, because we have to go that way." She pointed east and smiled.

"We've been going out of our way to lose them?" I asked.

"A couple of hours, maybe," she admitted. "We'll make it up."

"How?" I asked.

She grinned and said, "We just have to travel a little faster, that's all."

21

After dark I started to wonder if Chief Ryder had done me a favor, after all.

"Andy, are you sure you know the way?" I asked during a rest stop.

"What's the matter?" she asked, grinning, "you starting to wonder if we're lost?"

"I'm just wondering when we're going to get where we're going," I said. "I'm tired of being food for the insects."

I was also tired of being dirtier and smellier than I'd ever been in my life. Her face was once again as grimy as it had been the day I met her. Her clothes were damp and sticking to her, and I could see the points of her round little breasts. She noticed where I was looking and put her hand against her chest.

"Don't go getting any ideas, Clint," she said.

"Out here?" I said.

"Anywhere."

"Look, the only idea I've got is to get where we're going and take a bath."

"Another hour should do it," she said.

"Only an hour?" I said. "Then why are we sitting here wasting time?"

"Because you looked tired enough to drop."

I stood up and said, "Lead on, little girl. I can go as long as you can."

"Maybe we'll find out, sometime," she said, and started walking.

I stared after her, wondering if I'd heard her right. Now who was getting ideas?

22

It was just about an hour later when we broke through the trees and swamp into a clearing, and I couldn't believe what I saw.

Rising up out of the midst of the bayou was a beautiful and elegant plantation house, its classical white columns shining in the moonlight.

"Nice little place, huh?" Andy asked, watching me. "You're impressed, aren't you?"

"Surprised is more like it," I said.

"Come on, let's go inside," she said.

The closer we got to the house, the dirtier I started to feel. I figured the first thing I'd ask Martel for would be a bath. I followed Andy up to the front door, which she opened without knocking.

"Hey," I said, "do you always go into people's homes without knocking?"

She laughed at me and said, "Come on."

I followed her in and she closed the massive door behind us. The inside of the house was in keeping with the southern grandeur of the outside.

"I hope Mr. Martel doesn't mind—" I started to say, but I was cut off by a booming voice from behind.

"Andrea!" the voice called out.

I turned and found a tall, well-built man bearing down on us. Then I looked at Andy. They were both smiling broadly at each other, so it was obvious that they knew each other.

"Paul," she said, and it appeared that I had finally found Paul Martel.

The man opened his arms and took "Andrea" into them, and they hugged each other. He didn't seem to mind the dirt and grime at all.

Andy had a totally new look on her face, one I had never seen before. She was starry-eyed, and I had to assume that she was in love with Paul Martel. I wondered how his wife felt about that.

"You've been gone a long time this time," he scolded her, holding her at arm's length now. "Even with all of that dirt on you, you're prettier than a palomino pony."

All of a sudden, beneath all of the dirt and sweat, Andy the guide turned into Andrea, the young lady, and she shyly dropped her eyes to the ground.

She had forgotten all about me.

Martel, on the other hand, looked at me and said, "I'm Paul Martel. Are you a friend of Andrea's?"

"Oh, Paul," Andy said, suddenly coming to her senses again, "this is Clint Adams. He paid me to guide him here to you."

"Is that a fact?" he asked. He moved around her and extended a large hand towards me. As we shook, he examined me critically, and I had the feeling that Joey Revere had not delivered my message to his boss.

"You'll excuse me for asking, Mr. Adams,"

Martel said, "but I have some cause to be careful about men who are looking for me."

"I know about your house in New Orleans," I told him.

"Then you won't mind if I ask you why you're looking for me," he said.

He was as tall as me, but broader in the chest. He was in his early forties, but had kept himself in excellent shape. He was also an extraordinarily handsome man.

"Didn't your man, Revere, give you my message?" I asked.

"Joey?" he asked. Shaking his head he said, "He didn't say anything about a message. All he could talk about was how a stranger on a big black horse had gotten lucky—" He stopped short there, as if he'd just realized something.

"Was that your horse that beat me?" he asked.

"I'm afraid it was, and there was no luck involved," I assured him.

"He's got a beautiful horse, Paul," Andy said.

"I'm sure Joey was just trying to save face," he said, smiling at Andy. "Still," he said, turning back to me, "I'd like an answer to my question."

"Why I came to New Orleans to look for you?" He nodded and I said, "I came here from Washington. Your uncle wanted me to deliver a package to you."

"My uncle . . ." he said, and then nodded to himself. He turned to Andy and said, "I think you'd both like to take a bath. Andrea, why don't you show Mr. Adams where everything is, and then show him where he can sleep tonight. The largest guest room, I think."

"Yes, Paul."

"Mr. Adams," he said, turning to me again, "perhaps we had better talk in the morning."

"As you wish," I said.

"Good night, then. Have a good night's rest."

He turned to walk away and I called out to him.

"Mr. Martel."

"Yes."

"We were followed, at least part of the way here," I said. "I don't know if they were after me or you, but I think you should take some precautions."

He looked thoughtful, then said, "I think that is a very good suggestion. Good night."

"This way," Andy said, as Martel left the room.

I followed her to the large stairway and said, "You and he seem to know each other very well."

"We should," she said. "He's married to my sister."

"Then—"

She turned and smiled at me and said, "Yes, I live here, too."

"No wonder you knew the way," I said.

"Don't be mad at me," she said.

"I'm not," I assured her.

We started up again, but she turned and put one small hand against my chest.

"I still want to get paid, though. I might live here, but I make my own living."

"Don't worry," I said. "I'll pay you."

She showed me where the bath was, and then where the large guest room was.

"I'll see you in the morning, for breakfast," she said, at the door. "In the morning you can meet my sister, Michelle."

23

After a bath and a good night's sleep, I felt human again. You never know how clean "clean" really is, and how good it feels, until you've been really dirty—"bayou dirty" as Andy called it.

Early the next morning I was getting dressed when there was a knock at the door.

"Good morning," Andy said, and I barely recognized her. This was the greatest transformation yet.

"I've come to take you down to breakfast," she said. Her high-necked dress, plainly outlining her small, round, pert breasts, was pink, as was the ribbon in her clean hair. She was about to say something and I cut her off by getting there first.

"No ideas," I said, and she smiled.

"Are you hungry?" she asked.

"Starved."

"Then let's go."

She linked her arm through mine and we went down to breakfast together.

I still wanted to ask her if her sister Michelle was Michelle Bouchet, but I resisted. As we entered the room where breakfast was being served, I felt my stomach clench, but she wasn't seated at the table. Martel was there alone.

"Where's Michelle?" Andy asked.

"She'll be down shortly." Martel had just a slight french accent, which I'm sure would have made him that much more attractive to women.

"Sit down, Mr. Adams. Enjoy your breakfast."

There was no way I could have avoided enjoying my breakfast. There were several plates on the table, containing eggs, bacon, ham, potatoes and crepes. There was also plenty of hot, strong coffee, and I helped myself to that first.

Andy sat down and ate some eggs, but that was about all she would touch. She was a totally different person when she was around her brother-in-law.

"You saw my house in New Orleans, Mr. Adams?" Martel asked.

"What was left of it," I said. "In fact, I was shot at while looking at it."

"Indeed?"

I outlined briefly what had happened, and he said, "It would seem that house was bad luck for both of us."

"Worse for you than me, but I can agree with that," I said.

"You'll be happy to know that, if indeed you were followed, you were able to throw them off your trail. They have not shown up here."

"It was Andy's doing that we got rid of them," I said, and he seemed to flinch when I called her that.

"Andrea is very good at what she does," Martel said, adding, "although we wish she wouldn't do it so much and would stay at home more."

"I have to earn my own way, Paul, any way I can," she said.

"So you have said before," he remarked. "Your sister and I still wish you would change your mind"—and he looked at me as he finished—"but our Andrea has a mind very much her own."

"I've noticed," I put in.

"Andrea, dear," he said, "why don't you go up and speak to your sister. Tell her that our guest is waiting anxiously to meet her."

"All right," she said. "Excuse me."

When she had left the room, Martel said, "She is a puzzlement to me, that girl. I see the way she dresses when she leaves here, and I cannot understand her reasoning. It is as if she is hiding her loveliness from the outside world."

"She is very pretty," I agreed. "I hadn't noticed that until today."

"It runs in her family," he said, looking proud. "My wife is a very beautiful woman."

I tried to continue to enjoy my breakfast, but I kept glancing at the doorway, waiting for "his" Michelle to come in, to see if she was "my" Michelle, as well. I was becoming increasingly convinced that she was.

"How is the breakfast?" Martel asked me.

I jerked my eyes from the doorway, hoping he hadn't noticed me looking that way, and I said, "It's delicious. I'm grateful to you."

"I'm glad you're enjoying it," he said. Then he leaned close to me and said, "Do you have the letter?"

I hesitated a moment, touched by doubt for the first time since meeting him. There was no question, however, that this was the man who had been described to me.

"I can understand that you would want to be

sure," Martel said, "but you should be in possession of enough information to decide that I am who I say I am."

"All right," I said, putting down my fork. "Yes, I have the letter."

"Where is it?"

"It's up in my room, well hidden."

"Good. We will find an opportunity later for you to pass it on to me, and then your part will be finished."

I was about to argue that point, but he looked up at the doorway and the serious look on his face was replaced by a smile. I was amazed at how easy it was for him to switch expressions so convincingly.

"Darling," he said, standing up. "It's about time you decided to grace us with your presence."

I stood up, but deliberately did not turn around yet. I couldn't control my expression as well as Paul Martel could. I was afraid that if his wife proved to be the woman I knew as Michelle Bouchet, my feelings would be clearly reflected on my face.

"Mr. Adams," Martel said, "I would like you to meet my wife, Michelle Bouchet Martel."

24

"I am very happy to meet you, M'sieu Adams," she said.

Her expression was placid, but I thought I detected something akin to panic in her eyes.

"Mrs. Martel," I said, hoping that nothing showed on my face or in my voice.

"Come, darling," Martel said. "Sit and have breakfast with us."

Andy had already sat down and resumed picking at some eggs. Michelle glided over to the table and sat next to her husband, across from me.

"Just coffee," she told her husband.

"Darling, you haven't been eating enough," he scolded her. "Not since you got back."

"Everything is delicious, Mrs. Martel," I said.

She looked at me and said, "I'm sure it is, Mr. Adams, but all I wish to have is coffee."

"Allow me to pour it for you, then," I said.

"Thank you."

She had not met my eyes for more than a few scant seconds since she'd entered the room, and now as I poured her coffee for her she stared into the cup and did not look at me once.

For the first time since I had awakened

that morning to find her gone, I felt something other than puzzlement and frustration. I was beginning to feel angry.

How dare she affect me that way, and then return to her husband without a word of explanation. If she felt the least bit uncomfortable at my presence there, it served her right.

Conversation from that point on consisted of small talk between Martel and myself. The two ladies concentrated on *not* eating their breakfast.

When the meal was finished Martel stood up and said, "If you ladies will excuse us, we have some business matters to discuss. We'll be in the study."

Martel showed me into the handsome, booklined room. Now that I knew for certain that he was married to Michelle, I decided that I didn't like him much. Unfair to him, perhaps, but at that moment I wasn't concerned with what was fair and what was not. I was eager to conclude our transaction.

"Brandy?" Martel asked. I declined.

"Look, what did you mean by saying my part would be finished when I deliver the letter?" I asked.

"That *is* your job, isn't it?" he asked, pouring himself a snifter of brandy. Next, he opened a box of cigars and extended it towards me. I shook my head. He withdrew a long cigar from the box, snipped off the end, and put a flame to it, rotating it until he had it lit. "After all," he went on, "you are, if you will excuse the expression, just a messenger."

"Maybe I'll have that drink after all," I said.

He shrugged, poured me a brandy and then walked across the room to hand it to me.

"You brought me this," I told him, taking it from him. "Does that make you a messenger?"

He stared at me a moment, then said, "Very well, I concede the point to you. Still—"

"My job was to bring you the letter, and then make sure you recovered the gold safely.

"Are you to look after *me*, then," he asked, "or the gold?"

"Both. As I understand it, we can't get one without the other."

"Exactly."

"Then I guess for the time being," I said, "we're kind of like partners."

"I will not argue with the wishes of my uncle," he said, raising his brandy snifter to me.

He was too smooth, this Martel. I didn't trust him. I wondered again why he would be willing to recover the gold for the North. Was he getting a percentage from the government to turn it over? Maybe that was why Fenton said that the government couldn't pay me. They were already paying Martel.

"Another drink," he asked, "to seal the partnership?"

"No, thank you," I said. A few moments before, we had been on the verge of losing our civility, but it had been fully recovered.

"Well, then," Martel said, "I hope you'll make yourself at home as long as you're here. Perhaps you'll enjoy the view from our small veranda at the back of the house. You might like to sit there awhile to recover from your journey."

"Thank you."

"When you come down to dinner tonight," he said, as he was showing me out, "bring the letter with you. Afterwards, we will come here again for brandy and cigars, and you can give it to me.

"If the information you need is in that letter, when can we look forward to going after the gold?" I asked.

He looked thoughtful for a moment, then said, "We could leave tomorrow."

"Where is the gold?" I asked.

"We'll know that tonight," he said, "after dinner."

I had the feeling he already knew, but I decided I could wait a little longer. Something else was on my mind as I left that room, and that was how to get Michelle alone so I could talk to her.

When I got back to the dining room, everybody was gone, and the table had been cleared. This room opened out onto the veranda, so I went out and sat down. I couldn't very well go searching the house for her. I was just going to have to wait for the right time, and the right place.

25

While I was dressing for dinner, I was still thinking about Michelle Bouchet Martel. In fact, she was occupying my mind so completely that I almost left the room without the letter. I picked up my rifle, stuck my little finger into the barrel, and slowly drew out the rolled-up letter. I smoothed it out as best I could, then refolded it as it had been folded before, put it back in the original envelope, which I had kept, and slipped the whole thing into the breast pocket of my jacket.

Now I was ready to go down to dinner, sit across the table from Michelle and try to pretend that nothing had ever happened between us.

I was the last one to come down. The others were already seated at the table, and were in some kind of a heated conversation when I entered and they all stopped talking.

They were all dressed as if they were going to attend a ball, instead of just eat dinner.

There was an awkward silence as I entered and took a seat, and it was broken by Andy.

"Well," she said, "this is the first time since we've met that I've been dressed better than you." It was true; my best suit was fancy enough for

Texas, but in these surroundings it was barely adequate.

Polite laughter gave way to polite conversation as the dinner was served by Williams, the manservant. Aside from him, there was a maid and a cook, and they were the only other people in the house that I was aware of.

After dinner the two sisters—who, I noticed, spoke to each other only rarely—went out onto the veranda in such a way that I felt they were probably following instructions. Without a word, they both rose and excused themselves from the table.

Martel looked at me and said, "Shall we go to the study?"

For cigars and brandy?" I said. "Why not?"

I threw a last lingering glance at Michelle out on the veranda, then followed Martel out of the room.

In the study he didn't bother with the cigars and brandy. He turned and said, "Let me see it."

"No brandy?" I asked.

I took the envelope out of my pocket and handed it to him. He took it and said, "Help yourself."

I walked over to the brandy bottle, and behind me he said, "You've opened it?"

"Yes," I said, pouring myself a drink. "It wouldn't fit into my rifle barrel with the envelope."

"Did you read it?" he asked.

I turned around with a brandy snifter in my hand and said, "If I say no, will you believe me?"

He stared at me for a moment, then said, "In your rifle barrel, eh? Clever," and then took out the letter and started to read.

When he was through he said, "I'll take that drink, now."

I poured him one and brought it over to him.

"So? How does it look? When do we go?"

"I have to make arrangements," he said. "We'll leave day after tomorrow."

"Are we going back to New Orleans?"

"No," he said. "We'll keep going north, through the bayou. If all goes well, you won't have to go back to the city at all."

"My horse—" I started to say.

"That will be taken care of," he assured me. "Your horse will be waiting for you when we come out of the bayou."

He took the drink from me and put the folded up letter in his jacket pocket.

"Drink up, Mr. Adams," he said. "Our uncle is going to be very happy with both of us before this is over."

"What about your wife," I said, "and your sister-in-law?"

"They will be coming with us," he answered. "Again, if all goes well, I won't have to come back here, either. He raised his glass and added, "And I expect things to go very well."

"I can't help but wonder why you're doing this," I said.

"You mean, because I fought for the South against the North?" he asked.

"Yes."

"The South was defeated, Mr. Adams," he explained. "It is dead. Contrary to popular opinion among most southerners, it will never rise again. Why, then, should all that gold just sit there in the ground, doing no one any good?"

"That's an admirable attitude," I said. I didn't necessarily believe it, I added to myself, but it was admirable.

"We had better all get some rest tonight and tomorrow," he said. "We have a long trip ahead of us."

"To where the gold is buried," I said, and he nodded. "Where is the gold buried, anyway? Where are we going?"

He took his time answering, finishing his brandy first, and then he said, "We're going to Georgia."

26

The next day we found out that the men who had been following us through the bayou didn't give up that easily.

Apparently, Martel decided to have breakfast on the veranda, the last day in his bayou house. We were all present, and William was serving coffee when we heard the shot. The bullet hit William; I dove from my chair and grabbed Michelle, taking her to the floor with me. Andy and Martel were about a heartbeat behind me at hitting the floor. William had beat us all, but when he hit the floor, he was dead.

Intuition is a funny thing, but mine has been something over the years that I have put great stock in. Andy had stopped by my room that morning to tell me that we were to have breakfast on the veranda. I had not been wearing my gun in the house, but that morning I had decided to do so, perhaps because I knew we would be eating out in the open.

I was aware of Michelle's soft body beneath me, but I couldn't take the time to enjoy it. I drew my gun and scrambled over to the wall, which was waist high. As I peered over the wall, I saw one man with a rifle between the house and the edge of the bayou, and then I saw another farther back. I thought I spotted a third coming out from the trees, but couldn't be sure.

"How many do you see?" Martel asked. There was no surprise or shock in his voice.

"I see two for sure, maybe a third," I said. I could still see the man with the rifle. He was apparently waiting for someone to stand up, so he could get off another shot.

There was something familiar about his hat, though . . . and then I suddenly realized who it was, and who had probably been following us: my four poker buddies from the Abilene saloon.

"Do you have a gun?" I asked Martel.

"Not out here," he answered. "I'll have to go inside and get one."

"Do it, then," I said. "I'll cover you."

"I can go out the front—" he started to say.

"Check it out," I told him. "I think you'll find we're covered from the front, as well."

He scrambled along the floor for the doors leading into the house, and I kept an eye on the man with the rifle, who I thought was Deke Mason. That meant that he had to have Lon Carter, and the Fletcher brothers with him.

I heard movement behind me and said, "Both of you women stay down," without looking at them.

"I've got my derringer," Andy said.

She was wearing a dress, so I didn't know exactly where she had been wearing it, but I said, "It's no good at this range. Stay down."

After a few minutes, Martel came scrambling back out, carrying a rifle and wearing a six-gun. He came over and positioned himself next to me.

"What's out front?" I asked.

"One man."

"See the one with the rifle?" I asked.

"Yes, I see him."

"Look farther back, a few yards behind him. See another one?"

At the same time we saw another man's head, and he said, "Yes, I see him."

"That's three. If it's who I think it is there's got to be a fourth one."

"Who are they?" he asked.

I explained briefly about the poker game, and then explained that they had probably been the ones following Andy and me.

"But you've only seen three, so far?" he asked.

"That's right."

"Maybe they lost one in the bayou," Andy spoke up, "trying to keep up with us."

I looked at Martel, and he said, "That's certainly a possibility."

"Well, let's play it as if there were four," I suggested, "and we just can't find the fourth one."

"What do you think they want?" he asked. "Are they out for revenge against you, or do you think they know about the gold?" He asked me in a low tone, trying to keep the women from hearing.

"I don't see how they could know," I said. "I think they're out to salvage their pride by killing me for making them back down."

"They've come a long way for revenge," he said.

"Yeah, I know it."

Still, it was the only explanation I could think of. They couldn't have possibly known about the gold, and even if they did, what would killing everyone accomplish? They couldn't believe that the gold was in the house.

I stuck my head up to take another look, and the man I thought of as Deke Mason fired a shot, which struck the outside of the wall, underneath my chin. I saw the man's head from behind him, and it was moving to my left. I had a feeling that whoever that was—Carter, or one of the Fletchers —he was moving around to the side of the house.

"Let me have that rifle," I said.

Martel hesitated, but then obeyed.

"What are you going to do?"

"Watch."

I held the rifle so that I could aim and fire in a split second. Holding it that way, I watched the head of the man who was moving. In order to get around to the side of the house, he was going to have to come out in the open for a brief moment. I hoped to pick him off when he did.

"Adams—" Martel started, but I shushed him, not wanting to ruin my concentration. Obviously, whoever the man was, he thought he was out of sight. I watched his head as he stopped moving for a second, and then suddenly there he was, running in the clear. I moved fast, bringing the rifle up, moving with him and squeezing the trigger, ignoring the fact that Mason was firing at me.

In the open the man looked like Lon Carter, and as my bullet struck him he screamed, clutched at his chest and went down.

"You got him!" Martel said.

"Yeah," I said, sitting down with my back to the wall, "but I think they got me, too."

I put my hand up to my right shoulder and it

came away with blood on it. One of the shots Mason had fired while I was holding on Carter had struck me on the top of the shoulder, and passed on.

"How bad?" Martel asked.

"It's okay," I told him. The bullet was gone, and it had taken a small chunk of skin with it, but it wasn't serious.

I looked over at Michelle, who was watching me with frightened eyes, and then I looked at Andy, who for some reason was watching Michelle with an unreadable expression on her face.

"Martel!" a voice called out, and I recognized it as Deke Mason. "Martel!"

"Answer him," I said.

"What do you want!" Martel shouted back.

"All we want is Clint Adams, Martel," Mason said. "No harm will come to you or your ladies if you send Adams out!"

We all exchanged glances then, one by one examining each other's faces. I took a long look at Martel, wondering what was going on in his mind. He had the letter, so theoretically he didn't need me. He didn't know me all that well, so he didn't owe me anything.

I made the decision for him.

"Tell him okay," I said to him. "Tell him you took my gun and you're sending me out."

"No!" one of the women said; I couldn't really tell which one it was.

"Go on, tell him," I told Martel.

"I've taken Adams's gun, and I'm sending him out," Martel called out.

"We're waiting," Mason called back.

"What have you got in mind?" Martel asked me.

"Andy, throw me that derringer."

Suddenly it was clear what I was planning on doing, and Andy quickly produced her little gun and tossed it to me. I handed Martel the rifle and my gun and said, "Keep your eye on me, and move when I move. If the man from the front shows up, you'll have to take care of him. Give Andy a gun and let her watch for the fourth man, just in case he's out there somewhere."

"I'm waiting, Adams," Mason called out. "I got a deck of cards out here. We're gonna finish our game."

I palmed the derringer, and then stood up. I held my hands over my head, one in front of the other.

"That's it," Mason yelled, "come ahead."

"Good luck," Martel said.

As I climbed over the low wall I heard Andy scrambling across the floor to take up her position.

I started walking towards Mason, hoping that he would want me to reach him before killing me. I would have to be damned close to him for that derringer to be of any use.

When I reached him he stood up, laughing.

"Well, well," he said, "it's Mr. Back-to-the-wall Gunsmith. Look at him, without a gun—"

"Wrong, Mason," I said, cutting him off. I lowered my right hand and pulled the trigger on the little derringer. The tiny bullet struck him right in the forehead and he fell to the ground with a shocked look frozen on his face.

I heard some shots from behind me and turned to see what it was about. The two Fletcher brothers were there, one on each side of the house, and they were exchanging gunfire with the people on the veranda.

I hurriedly picked up Mason's gun and began running back to the house. I saw Andy stand up and fire a gun at one of the Fletchers, who fell to the ground. Martel and the remaining Fletcher brother were exchanging shots, but no one was hitting anything. When I got close enough I snapped off a shot at Fletcher, and he spun around from the force of the slug and fell to the ground.

I went over and checked him, and then did the same for his brother. They were both dead. After that, I checked on Lon Carter, the first man I had shot, and he was dead, too. Satisfied, I returned to the veranda.

Martel handed me my gun as I climbed over the wall, and I dropped Mason's gun and Andy's derringer on the table, in the midst of the breakfast plates.

"Are they all dead?" Martel asked.

"Yes."

"I'm afraid I'm not a very good shot," he said.

"That's all right," I told him, holstering my gun, "things turned out okay, anyway."

Sure, things had turned out okay, but the truth of the matter was that I wished he would have told me that before I decided to expose myself by walking right out to Deke Mason.

27

The incident moved our plans up one day. Martel decided that we should leave as soon as possible.

"When we reach the meeting point, we'll have to camp and wait for the horses to be delivered," he said.

I didn't argue the point. Vacating the house was a good idea, just in case Mason and the others had known about the gold and might have mentioned it to someone else.

"Who is delivering the horses?" I asked him as we gathered in the front hall with all of our supplies.

"Revere," he said. "I've already arranged it."

"What about your horse?" I asked.

"Michelle's Dancer?" he asked. "He is stabled in New Orleans. He will be among the horses Revere will bring, as well as yours. I'm looking forward to seeing this black horse of yours."

Michelle came back from the kitchen carrying a sack.

"I have taken whatever food we will need," she said.

"Good," Martel said.

Martel supplied bedrolls, mine being in the livery stable with Duke and my saddle. My saddlebags were in my room at the hotel, but I assumed that Martel would be very thorough, and that they would be delivered as well.

We divvied up the supplies so that Martel and I were carrying most of them. In addition, Martel was wearing a six-gun and carrying a rifle, as was I.

I knew Andy would have her little derringer, but I was surprised to see Michelle wearing a sidearm. It was also the first time I had seen her wearing anything but a dress. She was wearing a shirt, pants and boots, necessary apparel for the bayou.

"Can you use that?" I asked her, which was close to the most words I'd said to her at one time since we met.

"If I have to," she said.

"Michelle is a much better shot than I am," Martel said.

Which meant that I should have given *her* a gun back on that veranda instead of her husband.

"I think we'd better get going," I suggested.

"Right," Martel said.

We left by the veranda, all of us climbing over the low wall, and then with Andy at the point, we marched into the bayou, which was definitely not one of my favorite places.

28

The trip through the bayou was uneventful, and much shorter than my first. As we came out, night was just falling, and we set up camp.

"When should the horses arrive?" I asked.

"Tomorrow afternoon," Martel answered. "Perhaps he'll show up early." I couldn't imagine Revere showing up any earlier than he had to, but I kept my thoughts to myself.

Michelle and Andy quickly got things set up in order to cook dinner, and seemed to work fairly well together, although they still didn't talk all that much. We were all kind of dirty, and we broke out an extra canteen that we passed around and used to get cleaned up some.

The coffee was the first thing to be ready, and Martel and I each took a cup and relaxed while the women cooked dinner.

"Did you have any other trouble in New Orleans than what you've told us?" Martel asked.

I thought it over. Aside from the shooting incident, and the poker game at the Abilene, the only other person I had angered in any way was Martel's rider, Revere. That's what I told him.

"Revere likes to win," he said, "but he's loyal

to me. I don't think we should have any trouble from here on."

I hoped not. I wanted to help Martel recover the gold, get it delivered to Washington, and then wash my hands of the whole thing.

"How are you going to get this gold to Washington?" I asked. "How much of it is there?"

"I have a plan for delivery," he assured me, "but let's make sure it's there first."

I stared at him and said, "Do you have some reason to believe it might not be there?"

"I had certain information, without the letters," he explained. "All I needed was the information that it contained to put together with what I already knew in order to locate the gold exactly." He leaned forward and said, "If I can do it, why couldn't somebody else?"

"What was your information?" I asked.

He thought a moment, then shrugged as he figured there was no harm in telling me.

"I knew that the gold was buried somewhere in the southern region of Georgia," he said. "The information in the letter, which was compiled by some member of the secret service, helped me to pinpoint the location exactly."

"How did you know it was in Georgia?"

He hesitated, then said, "I was a colonel in the Confederate Army—even though I could not shoot very well—and I was in charge of a platoon that delivered a portion of the gold to Georgia."

"A portion of it?"

"The gold was collected from all over the confederacy, and delivered to Georgia, where one platoon took over and buried the entire fortune."

"So any man in that platoon will know where it is," I said.

"Almost all of them are dead," Martel informed me. "After they buried the gold, they were engaged by a platoon of Union soldiers. In the exchange, most of the Confederate soldiers were killed. Those few that were not killed were taken prisoner."

"There must be someone left alive," I reasoned.

"I assume that's where the information in the letter must have come from," he said.

"If someone in the Secret Service found one of those soliders, they wouldn't have needed you," I pointed out.

"That's true," he agreed. "So there must be another explanation as to how this information was obtained."

"I guess so."

"Dinner is ready," Michelle said, coming over to let us know.

"Thank you, darling," Martel said. I looked at Michelle and her eyes met mine. Martel got up and walked to the fire, leaving Michelle behind with me. For a moment I thought she was going to say something to me, but she bit her lip and turned to hurry after her husband.

After dinner we staked out our places to sleep around the fire, and I volunteered to take the first watch.

"I'll wake you in four hours," I told Martel. "This way the women won't have to take a turn."

"That's fine," he agreed.

The ladies, however, did not agree so easily.

"I can take a turn," Andy insisted.

"So can I," Michelle added.

"We'd rather you didn't," I told them both.

"I earn my own way, Paul," Andy told Martel.

"You ought to know that."

"I know, Andrea," he assured her.

"I'm afraid that you ladies are going to get stuck with all of the cooking chores on this trip," I told them. "So it's only fair that we take all of the watches."

"That seems to be a fair division of responsibilities," Paul Martel told his sister-in-law.

"If that's what you want, Paul," she finally said, and Michelle also agreed.

Andy went off to her bedroll while Martel and Michelle paired off on the other side of the fire. In the light cast by the flames, I could see Andy watching the two of them, and the look on her face was not a pleasant one.

Michelle's little sister was clearly in love with her brother-in-law, which made this whole trip a touchy situation. Then again, what could be touchier than the three of them living in the same house. Perhaps that was why Andy spent so much time away.

Then there was the way I still felt about Michelle, in spite of the fact that we had not had a moment alone together since I had found her again.

As far as Michelle's feeling for her husband, I couldn't believe that she was totally in love with him, not after the night we had spent together on the *Mississippi Queen*.

Before this trip was over, something was going to have to give.

29

I had a small hope that during the night Michelle would sneak away from her bedroll to talk to me, but it hadn't happened by the time it was Martel's turn to take the watch. I went to wake him and caught myself staring at Michelle, sleeping alongside of him. I shook myself and leaned over to wake him, then went back to my own bedroll to get some much needed sleep. We had a long trip that started the next day, and I was going to be as alert as I possibly could.

I was awakened in the morning by Andy, who didn't look too happy; she told me breakfast was ready, and I staggered to my feet, feeling as though I had only just fallen asleep.

"Coffee?" Andy asked, handing me a full cup.

"Thanks."

Martel and Michelle were on the other side of the fire, talking with their heads together. Once again I caught Andy staring at them with something less than affection.

"How long have you been in love with him?" I asked her.

She looked at me sharply, and for a moment I thought she was going to deny it, but instead she said, "Ever since I met him. You know, Michelle and I met him at the same time, but she's such a fine lady—"

"You could be a fine lady, too, Andrea," I said, using her real name.

"I try to be, when I'm around him," she said. "But it doesn't mean anything to him. He only sees me as Michelle's younger sister."

"I think he has a lot of honest affection for you," I said.

"I know he does, but it's as if he were my older brother. I don't want that from him." She looked over at them again and added, "As long as she's around, he'll never notice me."

I didn't know what to say to that.

"She's got you, too," she said, suddenly.

"What?"

"I see the way you look at her," she said. "I see the way all men look at her. You can't deny that you've got her under your skin, too."

I couldn't deny it, so I didn't. Instead, I extended my cup to her and said, "Shut up and pour."

30

It wasn't until after noon that we finally spotted some far off dust clouds.

"It's about time," I said, standing up.

The women started gathering up the supplies, but I said, "Take your time, he's still a ways off. He'll be here soon enough."

Duke was the easiest horse to spot, and I felt a rush of affection for the big boy when he came into view. Next to him was the big palomino, and neither of them had a rider, which wasn't surprising. If Revere had tried to ride Duke, he would've gotten himself thrown and stomped.

What was odd was that I could see two riders, not one.

"Was somebody supposed to come with Revere?" I asked Martel.

"No," he said. "No one."

"Maybe he picked up help along the way," I said. "Duke—my black—can be more than one man could handle."

"Yes," he said. "I suppose I could say the same for Michelle's Dancer, although Revere is his rider."

"We'll see," I said.

I watched as the riders got closer and closer, trailing horses behind them. Finally, when they got close enough, I recognized the other rider.

It was Jim Beam.

"I know the second rider," I said.

"Who is he?" Martel asked.

"He's been taking care of my horse in New Orleans. Seems he took his job real serious."

When they reached us I saw that Revere and Jim Beam were leading two horses each, with Revere holding the reins of the palomino, and Beam hanging onto Duke.

"I'm sorry, Mr. Martel," Revere said, dismounting, "But this . . . this—"

"Forget it, Revere," Martel said. He walked over to the palomino and began to rub his nose.

I went over to Duke, and while he nuzzled my hand, I asked Beam, "What brings you out here?"

"You didn't think I'd let him take Duke just like that, did you?" he asked, dropping to the ground from his horse. He came up close to me and said, "Revere was going to take Duke and the palomino and light out. I came with him to make sure the horses got where they were supposed to go."

"Good boy," I said. I looked over at Martel and wondered what kind of story Revere was telling him.

"You might as well head back," I told Beam. "We'll be heading out right away."

"I got nothing waiting for me back there, Clint," Jim said. "I hope you don't mind if I ride along a ways."

I clapped him on the shoulder and said, "Hell, I don't mind at all. You're welcome."

Martel came over to us now and began to inspect Duke. I could see by the look on his face that he was impressed.

"He's magnificent," he said.

"Don't try to touch him," I warned, when he looked as if that was exactly what he was going to do. "You're liable to lose your hand."

Revere held up his left hand, which had a handkerchief wrapped around it, and said, "That horse is loco. He almost took *my* whole hand off."

"He ain't loco," I said. "He's just particular about who touches him. . . . And he don't like vermin."

Revere gave me a glare but I turned away from him and ignored him.

"Would you sell him?" Martel asked.

"Would you sell one of your arms?" I asked back.

He smiled, looked longingly at Duke, and then looked over at his own horse.

"I understand," he said. "I think we had better get moving."

"Is Revere coming along?" I asked.

"Yes."

"So's my man," I said. "This is Jim Beam."

Martel looked at Jim, who nodded, and then said, "All right. Let's go."

We mounted up, and then headed out with Martel in the lead. We had to travel through a small section of Mississippi, then on through Alabama before we would finally reach Georgia.

Martel wouldn't tell me where the gold was, he would only take me there.

I guess he trusted me just about as much as I trusted him.

31

Georgia

A week later we crossed the border from Mississippi into Georgia and made camp.

"How far?" I asked.

"We still have a substantial amount of riding to do," he informed me. "I'll let you know when we get there."

"Sure," I said.

Things had not gone the way I would have liked during the journey. It had gotten so that every night we'd sit in two sections around the fire. The women would cook, while Jim and I sat on one side of the fire, and Martel and Revere sat on the other.

"I don't like this," I said to Jim that night.

"What?"

"Martel and Revere have got their heads together every night," I said.

"Yeah, well, so have we. So what?"

"Well, I know I'm not planning to steal the gold," I said.

I had not been the one to tell Jim about the

gold. As it turned out, Revere had found out from Martel, and then let it slip to Jim. I also hadn't liked the idea of Martel telling Revere. I couldn't see any reason for it.

"You think Martel plans to take it for himself?" Jim asked me.

"I don't know," I said. "I just don't buy the idea of an ex-Confederate officer all of a sudden wanting to help the North dig up some confederate gold."

"The war's been over for a lot of years, Clint," Jim reminded me.

"I know it," I said. "I know it, but it just doesn't feel right to me. And why tell Revere about it?"

"Maybe he let it slip to Revere, the way Revere let it slip to me," he suggested.

I shook my head.

"That man never lets anything just slip," I said.

"I guess we'll just have to watch them, then," Jim Beam said.

"Yeah," I replied, doing just that over the campfire, and Martel was doing exactly the same thing. Who knew, maybe he figured that we were conspiring to steal the gold. I could only go by what I knew, that I had no intention of stealing it. And I hoped that Jim Beam didn't either.

"You're wondering about me, ain't you, Clint?" Jim asked.

"You a mindreader?" I asked.

He laughed and said, "I'm glad you didn't deny it. I don't know what I can tell you to make you trust me, Clint, but I hate the thought of you having to split your attention between them and me."

I hated it, too. I was starting to think that I'd

made a mistake letting him come along. All it did was give me something else to worry about.

"I didn't know about the gold when we left New Orleans," Jim said. "I only came because I was worried about Duke. On the way, Revere let it slip. I swear, Clint, that's the way it was."

The look on his face said that he wanted me to believe him, real bad. My only problem was, I didn't know the real reason why.

"All right, kid," I said. I didn't say I believed him, I just said, "All right."

32

We rode into Blue Mesa, Georgia just as darkness was falling, and put up our horses at the livery.

"I can't wait to sleep in a real bed," Michelle said, as we all walked to the hotel.

"I'd like a drink," I said.

"That sounds like a good idea."

"Why don't Michelle and I go to the hotel and register for all of us, while you men go and get your drink?" Andy suggested.

Michelle looked at her sister, but I said, "That sounds good to me."

"Me, too," Jim Beam said.

Martel agreed and Revere naturally went along with his boss.

"All right," I said. "We'll see you ladies at the hotel, for dinner."

"Fine," Andy said. She tugged on Michelle's arm until her older sister followed her.

At the saloon I told the bartender, "Two bottles and four glasses, at that table." I pointed to a corner table, and the bartender nodded.

We walked over to the table and I took the chair with my back to the wall. The others sat down around the table, and the bartender brought over the whiskey and glasses.

When we all had full glasses in our hands I asked Martel, "How close are we now?"

"Very close," he said. He drank his whiskey and refilled his glass, then said, "You seem to be very anxious about this."

"I don't like playing games," I said.

"Is that what you think I'm doing?"

"I'd like to get this thing over with so I can get back to my life," I said.

"You may leave any time you like, Mr. Adams," he reminded me. "I never claimed that I needed you to find the gold."

I didn't like the suggestion. Sure, he'd like me to take off and leave him alone with the gold. He probably figured that if I left, Jim Beam would leave with me, leaving him with only Revere and the women.

I just flat out didn't trust the man, which is why I was bound and determined to see the thing through.

"I'll stick around," I said, and he nodded to himself, as if that were the answer he expected.

"Revere," he said. "In the morning I want you to go to the livery and rent a buckboard, and a team of horses."

"How many?"

"Four," Martel answered.

"Then we're *very* close," I said. *Otherwise why would he want a buckboard and a team?*

"But that was what I said," Martel reminded me.

A team of four horses rather than two meant that there was a lot more gold than I had thought. That much gold could make almost any man greedy.

I poured myself another drink and drank it, leaning my chair back against the wall. I eyed Martel, who looked smug and self-satisfied, and Revere, who was watching his boss. Beam was keeping his eyes on all three of us. We were all watching each other very closely.

That's what gold can do to a man.

33

When I left the saloon, Jim Beam left as well, saying he wanted to go to the livery stable to check on the horses. Martel said that he and Revere would stay a while longer in the saloon. Revere just nodded his agreement.

I walked into the small hotel and said, "My name is Clint Adams. What room do I have?"

"Thirteen, sir," the clerk said, giving me a funny look I couldn't interpret. I was too tired to think about it, so I just shrugged, took my key and went up to my room.

As I unlocked the door and walked in, I became aware that somebody else was in the room. I drew my gun before I knew what was happening, and Andy sat up in my bed, staring.

"Jesus," she said.

"Sorry," I told her, putting up the gun, "but I didn't expect anybody to be in my room." I holstered the gun and closed the door behind me, then asked her, "By the way, what *are* you doing in my room?"

"Our room," she corrected.

"What?"

"This is our room," she said again.

"What are you talking about?"

"They didn't have enough rooms to go around, so we have to share one," she explained.

"We have to share one," I repeated. "You couldn't share one with your sister, and let me share a room with one of the men."

She made a face and said, "I couldn't share a room with Michelle." Then she threw the covers down to her ankles, revealing herself to be totally naked, and said, "Besides, would you really rather share the room with one of the men?"

I knew that Andrea was pretty, in spite of all of her attempts to hide it, but I was totally surprised by this. First, by the fact that she was even there in my room, doing what she was doing, and secondly, by what a truly lovely body she had. Her breasts were small, but they were perfectly shaped. She had wide shoulders, a very small waist, and slim hips. Her legs were beautifully formed, and she bent one leg at the knee, as if to show me how lovely it really was.

"Andy—" I started to say, but she cut me off.

"Andrea," she said. "Call me Andrea. Please, Clint, please, tonight I want to be a woman." Her eyes pleaded with me as she said, "Make me feel like a woman."

I walked to the bed and sat on it, then slowly ran one hand down the length of her body. She closed her eyes and shivered as I touched her. I moved my hand back up to her breasts, and then cupped each breast in a hand. I tweaked her nipples so that they blossomed, and a moan escaped from between her lips.

In repose, her face was more than lovely; it was enchanting. Her lips were full, like a rosebud, and

I leaned over them and kissed her gently. She moaned and put one hand behind my head as she opened her mouth and sucked my tongue in. Her other hand went down between us and began to feel the bulge in my pants.

"Please," she said, breaking the kiss, "please get into bed with me. I want you."

I stood up and undressed while she watched me, and she looked pleased when she saw my erect penis. She reached for it, stroking it with a feathery touch, and then I got into bed with her and held her slim, small body close to mine. She felt incredibly hot, as if she were on fire.

I kissed her again and it was as if she were trying to crawl inside of me. Her mouth was all over me, as were her hands. Finally she pushed me onto my back with surprising strength and climbed atop me.

"Easy," I told her. "Take it easy."

I held her by the hips and guided her onto me, and I slid into her nice and easy. She gave a groan of satisfaction and began slowly to rock up and down. Soon her tempo increased until she was riding me fiercely. I let her go, because she obviously needed this. She put her hands flat against my chest and began to grind herself against me. When her entire body began to shudder, I released myself into her, and her eyes widened as she felt me filling her.

"Oh God," she moaned aloud, and I couldn't help but wonder what room Michelle was in, and if she could hear it.

She slid off me then and lay down beside me with her head resting on my shoulder.

"Surprised, aren't you?" she asked.

"Pleasantly," I assured her.

She rubbed her face into my chest and said, "God, so am I."

34

The next morning, as we all ate breakfast in the cafe, I noticed that every time I looked at Michelle, she would give me an icy stare. It made me feel good, for some reason. She must have known that Andy spent the night with me—whether she'd been able to hear us, or she saw Andy leave the room, or perhaps Andy even told her—but she was obviously not happy about it.

It was the first honest reaction I'd been able to get from her since finding her at her bayou home.

Andy was a pleasant surprise in the light of day, as well as the night before. She did not turn into a clingy female after having slept with me, but rather remained her independent self. There were no great sighs, or cow eyes thrown my way, as would have been the case with most young girls after they spend a night with a fellow.

"Get the buckboard," Martel told Revere as we were just about finished with breakfast. Revere threw a regretful glance at his plate, which was not yet empty, but he stood up and left the cafe to obey his boss.

"We must get something straight, Mr. Adams," Martel told me over a cup of coffee.

"What's that?"

"From here on in, I am in complete charge. In fact, I would like very much to run this as if it were a military operation."

"Well, I'll tell you, Martel," I said. "I was never a soldier, and I was never one for taking orders like one. I'm willing to let you call most of the shots, but I'm not here to play soldier with you."

He stiffened slightly and glared at me, but said, "Very well, if that's the way you feel."

"That's the way I feel."

"Why don't you send your man to get the horses," he suggested.

"Jim is his own man," I replied. "Why don't you ask if he would mind getting them?"

Martel glared at me again, then threw a look at Jim Beam, who grinned at him.

"Come, Michelle," Martel said, getting up. His wife rose and followed him out the door.

"I don't think you and him are going to get along very well the rest of the way," Jim said.

"That's okay," I said. "I don't think we ever really did."

"Be careful of him, Clint," Andy said. "He's a dangerous man."

"Sure, Andy," I said. "I'll be careful."

She stood up and walked out, and as Jim started to do the same I put my hand on his arm.

"We've got to watch each other's backs, Jim. Do you have a gun?"

He hadn't been wearing one up to that point.

"In my saddlebags, but I'm not very good with it," he said.

"Just wear it. Hopefully, you won't have to use it, but I'd like it to be in plain sight."

"Sure. I don't have a holster, but I'll tuck it into my belt," he said.

"Good enough. Let's go."

We went to the livery to get our own horses, and Revere had the four horse team hitched to the rented buckboard.

"Who's driving the buckboard?" I asked Martel, giving him the chance to make a decision—a minor concession, considering our confrontation at breakfast.

"Revere will drive the rig," Martel said. To Revere he said, "Tie your horse to the rear." Then he turned to Michelle, who had already mounted up, and asked, "Would you prefer to ride in the buckboard, dear?"

"I'm fine," she told him.

"Then I suggest we get underway," he said loudly.

We moved out, with Jim Beam riding on the right side of the buckboard, and me on the left. Martel chose to ride point, with Michelle next to him, and I allowed him to, preferring to be behind him. Also, by riding next to the buckboard, I was able to notice that Revere, who didn't wear a gun, had a rifle underneath the seat of the buckboard. I hoped that Jim had noticed it, as well.

35

We were about three hours out of Blue Mesa when everything suddenly went black on me.

When I woke up later, it was hard to remember exactly what had happened.

I was lying on my back in the dirt, and Duke was pushing at my face with his nose. I suppose if he hadn't done so, I wouldn't have woken up for quite some time yet.

When I tried to sit up I saw stars before my eyes, and dropped my head into my hands. I felt something sticky and when I looked at my right hand, there was blood on it.

Pulling Duke over to me, I used one of his stirrups to pull myself to my feet. Then, leaning on my saddle, I removed my canteen and used some water to wash the gash on the right side of my head, then I took just a little into my mouth to wet my lips and throat.

I wanted to mount right up and take out after them, but my legs wouldn't cooperate. They suddenly felt very weak and I slid back down to a seated position.

What had happened? The last I remembered I was riding alongside the buckboard, watching Martel as he rode ahead of me, and keeping aware of Revere and his hidden rifle. Then . . .

Then I was on my back in the dirt, with Duke trying to wake me up.

I tried to think back and remember if I had heard a shot, or anything just before I blacked out. Then again, the gash on my head proved that I didn't just black out—not without help, anyway.

Somebody had struck me, but who?

Was Martel making his move for the gold? Someone—perhaps Revere, since he was the closest—had struck me on the head in order to leave me behind. Why, then, leave Duke behind as well? Unless the big boy had simply refused to go with them. Short of killing him, there was no way to make him leave me if he didn't want to. He was simply too powerful. Knowing the way Martel felt about horses, he wouldn't have killed Duke. Then why not kill me? That was a question that would have to be answered when I found them.

I tried standing up again, using the stirrup. I leaned against the saddle for a moment, then pushed away and tried walking. There was some dizziness, but it passed and I was able to stay on my feet.

I pulled Duke around, put my foot in the stirrup and mounted up. Once I got on his back there was a black wave of dizziness and nausea. I held on to the big boy's neck until it passed and I was able to sit up straight in the saddle. I took out the canteen, drank some more water, and then started tracking Martel.

Tracking wasn't one of my strong points, but with the buckboard traveling with them, it wouldn't be very hard, until such time as they moved to harder ground.

Riding along on the trail left by the buckboard, I wondered who it might have been who had kept Martel from killing me. And what had happened to Jim Beam? What had he done after I was struck down? Did they buy him off then, with a promise of some of the gold?

Or had they bought him off before?

Maybe I would find his body somewhere along the trail.

I hoped I would not . . . and I hoped I would. I had come to like the boy, but if he had been bought by Martel, I would have hated to have to kill him.

36

The next time I woke up I was lying in a bed.

For the second time in one day—at least, I hoped it was the same day—I did not remember blacking out. I looked around the room, trying to identify where I was, but I had never seen it before. All I could tell was that I was not in a hotel room. The room was much too personal for that.

I put my hand to my head and found a bandage there. I put my other hand underneath the covers, and found that I was naked. A look around the room told me that my clothing were not close at hand, and neither were my guns.

I pushed myself up onto my elbows, leaned to one side and used one hand to throw the covers back. I swung my legs around and planted my feet on the floor. I felt very hot and thirsty, and my first thought was to get up and get a drink. My second thought was to get up and get out of there.

I put both of my hands down flat on the mattress, then pushed, trying to get to my feet. I fell back onto the bed once, in a seated position, but then finally managed to stand up unsteadily.

I was standing there, teetering, wondering which way to go when the door opened and the woman walked in. My vision was a little hazy, but I got the impression of a full-bodied woman in her early thirties who seemed a little shocked at seeing me standing there.

"What are you doing up?" she demanded, rushing to grab my arm. "Back into bed," she commanded.

"Uh, yeah, sure," I said, because I felt that if I didn't get back into bed, I would probably fall down. I backed up until the back of my knees struck the bed, and then I sat down. She grabbed my legs and swung them up onto the bed, then proceeded to cover me up.

"You're not supposed to get up yet," she informed me. "The doctor was very firm about that."

"Where am I?" I asked.

"I'd answer you, but that's the third time you've asked me that since you got here. When you're awake for good, I'll answer all of your questions," she promised.

I frowned at her and wanted to tell her that I was awake for good, but suddenly everything seemed to close in on me.

At least this time I knew I was blacking out, even if there was nothing I could do about it.

The next time I woke up, she was sitting there looking so much the same as she had before, that I could have sworn I had only been unconscious for a few seconds.

"If I ask where I am," I said, "how many times will that make?"

She smiled and said, "Four, but you seem much better this time. Your eyes look clearer."

They also looked clearer from my end. I was able to see her face now. She was not exactly pretty, but she had a clean, freshly scrubbed look that was appealing. Also, beneath the simple dress that she wore, I could see that she had full, solid breasts and hips. I put her age at closer to thirty-five, this time.

"Okay," I said, "so where am I?"

Even my voice sounded stronger, so I figured I was awake for good, this time—I hoped.

"You're at my farm, just outside of Nolanville, Georgia. Your horse brought you here yesterday, with you just barely sitting in the saddle."

"Yesterday?" I asked.

"Uh-huh. I got you in here and then sent for the doc. You had a fever all night, but it's gone down. Can I get you anything?"

"I could use a drink, and then something to eat," I said. "And I could sure use a bath." Obviously, with the fever, I had done a lot of sweating, and I could feel it and smell it.

"I'll get you some food and something to drink," she said, touching my shoulder. "As for the bath, we can take care of that, later."

She left the room and came back shortly with a tray. On it was a cup with some cold water, and a bowl of soup.

She sat with me while I ate it, and I found out that she was a widow, who was running her ranch with one hand, a sixteen-year-old boy.

When I finished eating she asked how it was, and I told her truthfully that it had been delicious.

"But?" she asked, smiling.

"I could use something a little more solid," I said.

"You must be feeling better," she said. "I've got some stew on. I'll bring you some, and some bread." She took the tray from my lap, and her hand brushed against me unintentionally. She looked at me and asked, "Would you like some whiskey?"

"Very much."

She came back with the stew and we talked some more. Her name was Rhea Marlowe and she had been living there alone for the four years since her husband died, trying to make a go of it. She had done fairly well, and just a few months ago had been able to afford hiring the boy as a hand.

"That was great," I told her, as I mopped up the last of the stew with a piece of bread.

"I'm glad you're feeling better," she said, picking up the tray and brushing the back of her hand against me again. This time I didn't think it was unintentional. Had she been without a man for the entire four years since her husband's death?

"I've got some work to do," she said, "but I'll be back later and then we'll see about your bath."

"When can I leave?" I asked.

She frowned, but said, "The doctor will be back in the morning to look you over. You can ask him. Excuse me."

She went out and I realized that I had forgotten to ask about my clothes, and my guns.

Slowly, because I didn't want to pass out again, I sat up, threw the covers off, swung my feet to the floor and gingerly stood up.

Success. I didn't fall, and my head didn't start going in circles. I took a tentative step forward, then another, and I was walking across the room, still as naked as the day I was born.

As I reached the closed door I had been about to open it when I heard a woman's moan from the other side. It was a sound I recognized, and I didn't want to burst in on anything. Still, I was curious, so very carefully, I opened the door a crack so I could look out.

I saw Rhea Marlowe lying on a small cot, naked, and on top of her was the sixteen-year-old boy she had hired as a hand. It looked as if he were a little more than just a hand.

The boy was awkward, and she was apparently trying to guide him, but he didn't seem to be very good. He was tall and skinny and looked ridiculous lying atop the full-bodied Rhea Marlowe. She had his long, skinny erection in her hands and was trying to guide him into her, but he was so over-anxious that he kept missing. I could see by the look on her face that she was starting to feel very frustrated. Finally, he entered her and she tensed, a low, guttural sound escaping her lips. He began to pump, his skinny buttocks rising and falling only twice before he moaned out loud and spent himself. He lay limply atop her, then slowly stood up, not looking at her face.

"I'm sorry, Mrs. Marlowe," he said, getting dressed.

She looked at him sadly and said, "Don't be sorry, Toby. It's all right. Just . . . go back to work."

The boy nodded, finished dressing and then left the house. When she was alone and unobserved—she thought—Rhea Marlowe buried her face in her hands and started crying. After a few moments, she stood up, her proud, full body seemingly slumped over in defeat. She walked across the room to a basin of water, raised one leg onto a chair and began to clean herself.

I sensed that this wasn't the time to ask her about my clothes and gun.

37

It was more than an hour later when Rhea came into the room, carrying a familiar looking basin, a sponge and some towels.

"What's all this?" I asked, as she put everything down on a small table by the bed.

"This is your bath," she said, and reached for the covers. I held onto them when she tried to pull them down, and said, "What do you mean?"

"I don't want you to get out of bed," she said, "so I'll give you a bath in bed."

She pulled on the covers again, but I held onto them stubbornly.

"Come on," she said, "don't be shy. I'm the one who undressed you and put you to bed, remember?"

She reached for the covers again, and this time I let her have them. She pulled them down and for a split second, she just stood there, staring at me. I remembered what I had seen in the other room a short while ago, and felt a stirring in my loins.

"Turn over," she said. "I'll do your back first."

"All right."

I turned over on my belly and she dipped the sponge into the basin, wrung it out and began to scrub my back. She was very gentle, and occasionally, after running the sponge over me, she would do the same with her bare hand. As she leaned over me, I could smell the musky, woman scent of her, and the stirring I felt became stronger.

She worked her way down to my lower back, washing me in slow, circular strokes, and then she was at my buttocks. She paused briefly, then moved down and did my legs and feet. She took a towel and dried me off, and when I started to turn back over she said, "Not yet. I got to wash your butt."

She took the sponge and began to rub it over my buttocks, and then suddenly the sponge was gone and her hands were replacing it. First she just rubbed me, then she began kneading me.

"You're all tense," she said. I wasn't really tensed, I was just uncomfortable, lying there on top of a massive erection.

She continued to knead my butt, then her fingers began to trail along the crack between my cheeks. Suddenly, one of her fingers reached down and traced my testicles. I opened my legs to allow her better access, and she actually reached under me and cupped them. As she caressed them, she bent over and began to run her mouth over my behind.

Suddenly, her touch was gone and I thought I heard the soft rustling of clothing.

"Don't turn over," she said, huskily. "Not yet."

I felt two hard tips touch my back, and I realized that they were the nipples of her breasts. She was moaning now, rubbing herself over me, flattening her large breasts against my back.

"Turn over," she said suddenly, "for God's sake, turn over."

She moved off me and I turned over eagerly. My eagerness did not quite match hers, though. She was on me with the speed of a wildcat, pushing her breasts into my face, running her hands over me until they found what they were after, and then she hung on like her life depended on it.

I sucked on her breasts and she stroked my penis until neither one of us could take it any longer.

"God, it's been so long," she said, with her mouth against mine, "so damn long . . ."

I put her on her back and drove myself into her as deep as I could go. She cried out, then a look of pure joy came over her face as I began to move in long, slow strokes.

"Oh, my God, yes, that's it, that's what I've needed for so long," she said. She wrapped her powerful legs around my waist and brought her hips up to meet each stroke. I felt the rush building in my legs and wondered how long I'd have to control it. But as it turned out, she was ready when I was and we rode the wind together, with her tossing her head back and forth, laughing out loud.

When I rolled off her she buried her face in my neck and said, "Thank you, thank you."

"Don't thank me, Rhea," I said, running my hands over her breasts. "Don't ever thank any man for taking what you have to give, and giving in return. You deserve it."

She smiled at me, kissed me shortly and said, "I have to finish your bath."

"No—" I started, but she said, "Yes," and rolled out of bed.

Remaining naked, she took up where she left off. She kneeled by the bed and began to wash my chest.

"You don't have to do this," I told her, stroking her cheek.

"I want to," she assured me, then she said reverently, "Oh, I want to."

She finished my chest, skipped over my groin to do my legs, then dried me.

"Now," she said, with her eyes shining, and she began to run the sponge over my genitals. Slowly, my penis began to rise to the occasion again, and pretty soon she discarded the sponge, took me into her hands, lowered her head and touched her lips to the tip of my penis. She rubbed me all over her face, moaning and smiling, and then opened her mouth and took me in, rubbing her hands over my belly and chest as she sucked on me vigorously. Suddenly, I felt as if I was going to black out, but I wanted to stay awake to enjoy the end. I fought the closing darkness, and then suddenly I began to shoot my semen into her mouth, and she moaned and swallowed, caressing my testicles, squeezing them until she had every drop.

38

The doctor came the next morning and pronounced me to be surprisingly fit. I told him it was all due to Mrs. Marlowe's splendid care.

"Fit enough to ride?" I asked, then.

The old doctor fixed me with a squinty-eyed stare and asked, "What would you do if I was to tell you no?"

"I'd ride."

"There you go," he said. "Have a nice trip."

"Thanks doc," I said, and he waved, picked up his little black bag and left.

Rhea came in as I was getting dressed. She had washed my clothes, and when I woke up that morning, they had been draped over a chair, along with my gun.

"You'll be leaving now," she said.

"I'd like to stay, Rhea," I told her honestly, "but I've got some catching up to do, some debts to pay."

"I know," she said. "I'll give you some breakfast before you leave."

Sadly she turned and went into the next room. I stood there staring at the empty door for a few moments, sorry that there wasn't something I could do for her. I hated to leave her there on that farm, with only a sixteen-year-old kid for help and comfort, but there was nothing else I could do. I had to catch up with Martel and the others. I owed somebody for a bump on the head, and I aimed to pay off.

I finished dressing, then strapped on my gun and walked into the other room. She was at the table, putting down a plate of eggs and bacon, with some bread on the side, and a pot of coffee.

"Maybe you'll come back this way some time," she said, as I was eating.

"That's possible," I told her.

"If you're still alive, that is."

"Why do you say that?"

"You talked in your sleep, you know," she said, "when you had the fever."

"About what?"

"About somebody named Michelle. Is she your wife?"

"Someone else's wife," I said. "I don't have one."

"You never got married?" she asked.

"Got close once," I said. "But no, I never did."

"What happened?"

"My job got in the way," I answered, in between bites. "I was a deputy sheriff at the time. . . . A long, long time ago."

"Are you a lawman now?"

"No, I'm not. I gave it up."

"Then why do you have to follow these people?"

"What people?"

"The ones you talked about in your sleep. You said you had to catch up to them, and save the gold."

I stopped my fork short of my mouth and stared at her.

"Oh, don't worry," she said. "If there's gold involved, I won't mention it to anyone. You can trust me, Clint."

"Yeah," I said. "Maybe I can at that."

I finished up my breakfast and then went out to check on Duke and saddle him up. The kid, Toby Dean, kept giving me dirty looks when he thought I wasn't looking, so it was obvious he knew what had happened between Rhea and me last night. It was also obvious that he would not be particularly unhappy to see me leave.

I walked Duke around to the front of the house and found Rhea waiting with some supplies.

"Bacon, coffee—lots of coffee," she said, smiling. "Lots of other things."

"Rhea, you've got to let me pay you," I said. "For the food, the doctor—"

"You've already paid me, Clint," she said, touching my arm, "with something much more precious than money." She stood on her toes and kissed me softly on the mouth, a lingering kiss that was designed to make me drop everything and stay—and was almost worth just that.

She stared at me then, and I said, "I have to go, Rhea. I don't have a choice."

"I know," she said. "I understand . . . but there is something you should know."

"What?"

"They passed here. The people you're looking for," she said. "The man on the palomino, and the two women."

"What? When?"

"A day before you did."

"How many were there?" I asked. "Just the man on the palomino and the two women?"

"No, there were two other men, also. The very

beautiful one, is that Michelle?" she asked.

"Yes, that's Michelle, and the man on the horse was her husband."

"She doesn't love him," she said.

"What?" I asked. "How do you know that?"

"They stopped to freshen up; they bought some supplies from me. I watched them together, and she doesn't love him."

I shook my head slowly. "That's quite an assumption to make after just seeing them together—"

"A woman knows, Clint. She doesn't love him, but the other one, the younger one, she does."

"You're very observant," I said.

"Yeah. Anyway, they went south."

"South?" I asked. When I was with them, we had been traveling north. Why the hell would they cut south, unless going north was just to throw me off.

I looked south, trying to figure how far ahead of me they were. They had beat me here by a day, and I had been here two days, so they were three days ahead of me. Of course, they were moving fairly slowly, and I had Duke. If I rode all night, I might be able to catch up to them before they reached the gold.

That is, if they had not already reached it, recovered it, and rehidden it somewhere.

If that were the case, they could have been anywhere by now, even heading back to New Orleans . . . or to another country entirely.

"I guess I go south," I said to Rhea. "One step at a time."

39

After three days, the trail was very faint. Still, there were some indications that at least told me I was going in the right general direction.

It felt good to be back on horseback, even though I did feel a little weak. I owed it to Duke, though, that I was back on my feet—or his back—so soon. He had gotten me to Rhea Marlowe's ranch when I was unable to guide him. That was the kind of thing we'd always done for each other since we'd been together, which is why I could never sell him. I don't own him; we're partners, and we look out for each other.

"You did it again, big boy," I said, patting him on the neck affectionately. "In fact, I think this may put you one or two up on me."

He tossed his head to show me that he wasn't keeping count.

"I appreciate that," I told him.

I thought about what Rhea had told me before I left. From what she said, it didn't appear that Jim was a prisoner. That could mean that he was in on whatever was going on. Maybe not from the beginning, but he had left me behind, unconscious, just as they had, so that put him on my pay-back list. I was sorry about that. I had liked him, had even started to trust him a little.

As darkness fell, I started looking around for some sign of the direction they'd taken. I hoped they would keep going south, and not cut back again. I had to assume that Martel was no longer worried about me, and would have no further reason to double back.

In the darkness, I'd just continue to ride south, and hope that I was closing ground on them and not chasing something that wasn't even there anymore.

40

In the morning, as the sun started to come up I was fighting my own tiredness when I found something that woke me right up.

I found Jim Beam's body.

I spotted it from a distance away and felt a cold chill. I guess I sensed *what* it was; I just didn't know *who* it was.

I was afraid it might be Michelle.

I quickened Duke's pace and as we rode up on the body I could see it was a man, not a woman, and then I knew who it had to be.

When I dismounted and turned Jim over, I found that he'd been shot in the chest three times. I looked around, but there was no sign of his horse. He hadn't been as lucky as I had. Somebody or something had kept Martel from killing me, but Jim didn't have that luck. I went through his pockets, but they were totally empty. His gun was gone, too. The only thing they'd left were his clothes.

"Sorry, Jim," I said, standing up. "You should have stayed in New Orleans, tending horses."

I mounted up and continued south. At least finding Jim's body told me that I was heading in the right direction.

Either Jim had been a victim, or there had been a falling out among him, Martel and Revere, and one of them had killed him. I wondered how Michelle and Andy were holding up under all of this.

Maybe just about now, Martel was having trouble keeping one or both of them in line. I feared I just might find some more bodies along the way. Sure, they were his wife and sister-in-law, but this was gold we were talking about.

Gold.

41

Having been off my feet for so long, and then riding all night had finally caught up with me. The sun was on the way down when I eased Duke to a stop and dismounted.

"That's it, big fella," I told him. "If I don't lie down for a few hours, I'll fall down. We don't want to go through that again."

I walked Duke over to a small group of rocks, then took my bedroll down and threw it on the ground. I didn't unroll it, I simply lay down in the dirt with my head on it. I hoped to catch a small nap and wake up in a couple of hours. In my condition, though, I couldn't be sure that I wouldn't just conk out and sleep for two days. Still, I had to take the chance, otherwise when I did catch up to Martel, I wouldn't be able to do a damned thing.

"Relax for a couple of hours, big boy," I told Duke. "If I'm not up in two hours, give me a nudge." Who knew? Sometimes he acted almost human. I wouldn't have been surprised if he did nudge me awake in two hours.

I fell asleep almost immediately, only to be nudged a short time later, but not by Duke. The first thing I saw when I opened my eyes was the big black, and he looked agitated and . . . disappointed. My guess was that he had tried to wake me up—short of nudging me—and I had slept through his attempts.

It was the toe of a boot in my side that finally woke me up, and then the second thing I saw was the gun pointed at my face. The owner of the toe and the gun was the same person, and he also owned an ugly face that wore a tight smirk.

"Up, easy," he said, jerking the barrel of his gun in an upward motion.

As I moved to get to my feet, someone else stepped in behind me and relieved me of my gun. I hesitated, then continued to stand up. As I did, I looked over at Duke, and I could have sworn he gave his head a little shake.

"Sorry, fella," I said.

"Shut your mouth!" the man with the gun snapped.

Now that I was fairly well awake, I took a better look at him. He was still ugly, and he still had the gun on me, but now I also noticed what he was wearing: a Confederate uniform, with three stripes on his arm, indicating that he had been a sergeant.

"Look around," he told me. I obeyed, and found that there were four other men similarly clad, none of them wearing more than a single stripe.

"I suggest that you don't try nothing funny if you wanna keep breathing," the sergeant said.

"I'll go along with that," I said. "What's going on, anyway? Don't you fellas know that the war is over?"

The sergeant smiled widely now, revealing uneven, yellow teeth, and said, "That's what a lot of dirty northerners think, too." He turned to one of the other men and said, "Tie him up and get him up on his horse. We'll take him to the general."

"Who's the general?" I asked.

"You'll find out, but you'll find out faster if you don't talk until we get where we're going," the sergeant said. He walked up to me and placed the barrel of his gun against my chin.

"Until then, consider yourself a prisoner of the New Confederate Army."

They tied my hands, blindfolded me and hoisted me up onto Duke's back. We started to ride, and soon after that I lost track of time.

"How long will this—" I started to ask, but I stopped when I felt a gun dig into my ribs.

"Ask your questions later, friend," the sergeant's voice said, "when you talk to the general."

Obviously, I had stumbled onto a group of ex-confederate soldiers who, even after all the years that had passed, refused to admit that the war was over, and the South had lost. This wasn't the only such group to pop up in the years since the end of the war, but it was a bad time for me to run into them. Who knew when I'd be able to get away from them—or where Martel would be by that time.

What was this group doing in this area, anyway? Could it have been that they were looking for the gold, too? If so, who had found it, them or Martel?

Or had it been found at all?

I resigned myself to the fact that none of my questions would be answered until I was finally able to talk to the "general," so I tried to relax, and succeeded to such an extent that the inevitable happened.

I fell asleep.

42

I was awakened by someone dragging me down off my horse. I staggered when my feet hit the ground, lost my balance and fell. Unable to break my fall with my hands behind my back, I hit the ground hard enough to knock the wind out of me.

"Come on," I heard the sergeant's voice growl. "Get him up and put him away. I'll tell the general that he's here."

"Right, Sarge," another man's voice said.

I felt a couple of strong hands grab me by the elbows and the same voice said, "Up we go, friend," as I was yanked to my feet.

I was still trying to catch my breath as he pushed me along from behind to wherever it was he was supposed to "put me away."

Abruptly, I walked into something, banging my face. The man behind me laughed, reached past me and opened the door he had guided me into.

"Works everytime," he said, pushing me inside.

"Okay, pal, off with your blindfold," he said, pulling it free of my eyes, "and your ropes." He untied my hands and I started trying to rub some life into them.

"See you later, friend," he said, backing out.

"How much later?" I asked.

"Could be a few hours," he said. And then, just before he closed the door he added, "Or a few days."

I could hear him laughing uproariously as he locked the door and then walked away. Gradually, the sound of the laughter faded away and I was left totally alone.

The room was pitch dark, so I just stood still, rubbing my hands and wrists and letting my eyes become accustomed to the darkness. The feeling came back into my hands just as my eyes began picking out shapes in the room. I walked to what appeared to be a cot, felt it, satisfied myself that it was indeed a cot, then put it to the use for which it was there; I lay down on it.

I was satisfied, without checking it, that the door would be sturdy enough to keep me inside for as long as they wanted me. All that was left for me to do was to get as much rest as I could, so that if and when the opportunity to make a break arose, I would be able to take full advantage of it.

43

Time ceased to be a factor for me.

All I knew was that since I had been there the door had been opened twice, each time for a man to bring me a meal. Once it was dark, and the second time it was light. They removed the remnants of the first meal when they brought the second.

Two meals. What did that mean? If they were feeding me three times a day, it meant that I had been there approximately sixteen hours. If they were feeding me twice a day, then I had been there for a day. In the event that they were feeding me once a day, then I had been there two days, already.

I was awakened again by the sound of the door opening, and a third man came in with my third meal. Never the same man, I noticed.

"You asleep again?" he asked, putting down the tray of food. That meant that the other two had talked about me. "Ain't you nervous? Ain't you wondering what's gonna happen to you?"

"Can't do either if I'm asleep, can I?" I asked. Those were the first words I'd spoken since I'd been brought there. I was surprised at how clear and strong my voice was.

"You're a tough one, ain't you?" he asked, picking up the remnants of my second meal.

"Not me friend," I said, walking to the table to inspect what he had brought me in the light from the open door. "I'm just too tired to give a shit, right now."

He laughed dryly, then left, once again leaving me in the darkness. The meal was the same thing it had been before, some kind of stew that had too much salt on it again. I guessed that was to keep me from telling what was breakfast, what was lunch and what was dinner.

I wasn't very hungry, which led me to believe that a whole day had not gone by between meals. I figured they were feeding me twice a day, which meant I'd been there at least a day and a half.

Whoever the general was, he played a very good waiting game. I doubted, however, that he was spending the intervening time asleep, as I was. Maybe he was thinking about me more than I was thinking about him.

I hoped so, anyway.

I finished the meal even though I wasn't famished, because who knew when the general might decide to stop feeding me. I pushed the plate away and stood up, wondering how I felt. I thought about it, and then decided that I felt pretty good, considering the abuse my body had received over the last three or four days. I felt pretty good, but not as good as I wanted to. My head still ached a little.

I wondered why they hadn't been bringing me anything to drink with my meals, and that was when I realized why my food had been so heavily salted.

I was thirsty.

I was becoming more and more impressed with the "general" as time went by, however slowly.

But not impressed enough to lose any sleep over it.

44

The next time I woke up it was on my own, which was a good sign. I stood up, walked around the room and realized that I felt much better. My headache was totally gone; I felt strong and awake.

I was still thirsty, though. I sat on the cot and waited for my next meal to be brought. I didn't have long to wait. As the light flooded into the room from outside, I received a surprise for which I was not prepared: The person carrying the tray was Andrea Bouchet.

"Andy!" I said, my tone betraying the shock and surprise I felt. "How did you get here?"

"I'm not allowed to answer any of your questions, Clint. They'll all be answered when—"

"When I see the general," I ended for her. "That's all I've been hearing. When *do* I see the general?" I asked. "And who is he?"

She looked at me, her face expressionless, and said, "I'm sorry."

As she started to leave I called out, "How about something to drink, next time? The overabundance of salt is really doing the job."

She turned, looked at me, said, "I'll ask," and then left, pulling the door shut behind her. I listened as she locked it and walked away.

After I ate, I sat back and wondered how Andy had ended up in the camp of the New Confederate Army. I could only assume that Martel and the New Confederate Army must have all found the gold at the same time, and he, Michelle, Andy and Revere had been captured. It was even possible that it was then that Jim Beam had been shot and killed.

If the general of this New Confederate Army had the gold, maybe he had killed Marten and Revere, and kept the women alive for . . . other purposes. I remembered how Con Macklin had used the women in his camp when he had been building *his* own private army.*

The big question now was, why was I being kept alive? All I was doing was going through food—and salt—that his own men could have been eating. He must have had some kind of plan for me, but what?

Maybe Martel had given me up as a member of the secret service. If that was the case, the general might think I had some valuable information to help the rise of his New South. I might have to perpetuate that deception to keep myself alive long enough to figure a way out.

I started to concoct up things I could tell him to keep him satisfied. When—and if—I finally met him, I was going to have to size him up pretty quick in order to figure out what lies he would and would not believe.

I hoped he was only a mad *man,* and not a mad *genius*.

---

*Macklin's Women, Ace Charter Books, 1/82.

45

Being idle while awake was a lot harder than sleeping away the time. I tried going to sleep again, but I'd slept plenty and couldn't force myself to lie there and close my eyes.

I realized what the General had been trying to do, and if I had been awake all this time, I figured I might just be ready to go crazy by now.

After what seemed like hours, I heard the lock being taken off the door, but instead of a man—or Andy—with a tray of food, two men with drawn guns walked in. I recognized one of them as the sergeant who had brought me in.

"Let's go," he said to me, gesturing with his gun. "The general is ready to see you now."

"I hope I can at least get a drink of water," I said, getting up from where I had been seated on the cot.

"That'll be up to the general," he said.

Annoyed with the general, I said to the sergeant, "Does he tell you when and where to shit, too?"

"I've got a good mind to open your face with the side of this gun," he said to me as I walked up to him.

"Yeah," I said, "but the general wouldn't like it, so you won't," and I walked past him out into the sun.

I was staggered in that moment, not by any blow struck by the sergeant, but by the sheer, almost physical impact of the sun. I had been in that dark room for I didn't know how many days, and now the sudden reintroduction to the fierce sunlight was almost more than I could stand up to.

I covered my eyes with my hands and actually crouched, as if ducking away from a punch. The sergeant put his hand against my back and pushed, saying, "Let's go."

I moved forward, constantly prodded from behind by the sergeant, still shielding my eyes from the sun.

"He walks like an old lady," the man with the sergeant said, and I couldn't argue that. I was bent over, doing my best to keep the sun away from my eyes.

As we walked I was gradually able to adjust my eyes enough to see that we were walking across some sort of compound. There were men standing all around, all wearing Confederate uniforms, watching our progress across the compound.

Eventually, we walked into a shadowed area and I was able to take my hands away from eyes and look around. We seemed to be inside a small fort, and standing around in the compound I counted about fifteen men.

"In there," the sergeant said, pointing to the doorway of the wood-framed building in front of us. The sign on the building said COMMANDING OFFICER'S OFFICE.

I ascended the three steps and stopped while the sergeant reached in front of me to open the door.

"Inside," he said, giving me a push.

I entered the office and found myself looking at Joey Revere, in a Confederate uniform.

"Here he is," the sergeant said.

Revere looked up from his desk and smirked at me. I saw that he was wearing captain's bars.

"Aren't those bars a bit heavy for a little guy like you?" I asked him.

He stood up to his full five foot five and regarded me coldly. The sergeant, standing next to me, stifled a laugh, and for that he drew a cold look, as well.

"You would be wise to be a bit more respectful, Adams," Revere said. "You are a prisoner of war, and as such should watch your tongue."

"What war?" I asked. "The only war I remember ended over six years ago." I leaned forward and added in a mock low voice. "You lost."

"We choose not to accept that verdict," Revere said, proudly.

"Well, that's the way it's going to go down in history," I told him. "One loss for your side."

Revere smirked again and said, "You'll sing a different tune when the New South rises."

"Horse shit," I said.

"Why don't you tell the general he's here?" the sergeant suggested.

Revere threw the man a sharp look and said, "Let's remember who outranks whom, Sergeant."

"Yes, sir," the sergeant said wearily.

Revere went to another door, knocked, opened it and walked in.

"What an asshole," the sergeant said to no one in particular.

"At least we agree on that," I said.

"He thinks because he's a little butt kisser—" the sergeant started to continue, but when the door opened again, he stopped.

Revere stepped out and said to the sergeant, "Bring him in."

"Let's go," the sergeant told me, giving me another push. I guess we weren't friends anymore.

I walked through the door to the office of the commanding officer, the man who was engineering the rise of the New South. I wasn't surprised when I saw the man behind the desk. Revere's presence had given it away.

The "General" Paul Martel stood up behind his desk.

46

"Should I be surprised, Martel?" I asked him.

"General Martel," he corrected me, standing straight and tall.

"You've given yourself a promotion, I see."

"One that should have been given me long ago, Mr. Adams," he replied.

I looked around the office and saw a few bottles and a decanter on a table against the right wall.

"How about a drink?" I asked him.

"Of course," he said. He looked beyond me then and said, "You may go, Sergeant. Close the door and wait outside."

"Yes, sir."

As the sergeant left the room, Martel walked to the table, picked up the decanter and said, "Brandy?"

"No," I said, "something stronger. Whiskey."

He turned and gave me a disapproving look, then poured himself a glass of brandy, and me a glass of whiskey. He walked back behind his desk and put my glass down.

"That one's yours," he said. "You can have it after we talk."

"Talking is thirsty business," I reminded him.

"Yes, I know." He sipped his brandy with a flourish and set his glass down next to mine.

"What do you want to know?" I asked him, as calmly as I could. My mind was racing. I knew I had to throw out most of the lies I had been planning to tell, because Martel would know better than to believe me.

"Actually," Martel went on, "I only have one question for you to answer, and then you can have the drink."

The son of a bitch knew how thirsty I was, and how much I wanted that drink, even though I had tried to be as nonchalant as I could while asking for it.

"What question is that?" I asked.

He put both his fists on the desk and leaned towards me, saying, "Where is the gold?"

"*What?*" I was incredulous.

"You heard me, Adams," he said. "Where is my gold?"

"*Your* gold?" I asked.

"The New South's gold," he said, correcting himself.

"I don't know where the gold is, Martel," I told him. "I thought you had it. You don't think I got there first, do you? Not after you left me behind? And how would I even know where to go? You never showed me the letter."

"Do you take me for a fool?" he exploded, standing up. "Do not make that mistake, Adams. I am no longer the Paul Martel who you met. I am General Paul Martel, of the Army of the New South."

"The New Confederate Army," I said, nodding. "I've heard of it. Small outfit, ain't it?"

"You may laugh," he said. "You may scoff. Yes, we are small now, but when I find that gold, we will grow, we will become powerful, and we will take the South back!"

I applauded him, and he looked at me as if I had smacked him in the face.

"You should be on stage," I told him.

Abruptly he reached behind him and came out with a long saber, which he held menacingly in his right hand.

"You are lucky, my friend, that I don't choose to kill you now. But I need that gold."

"I told you, Martel, I don't know where it is."

"You do!" he insisted. "You read the letter that you were supposed to deliver, and you figured out where the gold was. Then you substituted the forgery that you delivered to me." He pointed the saber at me and said, "You may not have the gold, sir, but you know where it is."

"Wait a minute," I said, shaking my head. "Let me see if I've got this straight. When you got to wherever it was you were going, there was no gold there?"

"You know there wasn't," he said. "You switched letters."

What I did next must have shocked Martel, because it shocked the hell out of me. I started laughing.

"Are you mad?" Martel demanded, staring at me. "Stop that, man, or I'll have you shot!"

I was too far gone to be affected by threats. I just kept on laughing while he stood there and gaped at me.

"The man's mad," he said to himself.

"No," I finally managed to say. "No, I'm not

mad. I should be," I added, "but I'm not. I think it's all very, very funny."

"What is so funny?" he demanded.

"You really don't know, do you?" I asked him.

"Don't play games with me, Adams," he said.

"I'm not the one playing games with you, Martel," I told him. "It's the United States government. It's Grant and the Secret Service. They're playing games with both of us."

"What are you babbling about?"

"They never bought you for a minute," I explained. "But they didn't want to take the chance that they might be wrong, so they decided to bait you with a phony letter, and see if you would try to make a move on the gold. They set us both up," I said, shaking my head. "I guess I should be pretty angry. Maybe I will be later on, but right now the whole thing strikes me as being real funny."

He glared at me for a moment, with that big pig-sticker in his hand, and then he bellowed, "Sergeant!"

The sergeant came rushing in and Martel told him, "Take him back. Take him back until I decide how to kill him."

"You think it over, Martel," I told him. "You'll see I'm right. You've been had, and you've given yourself away for nothing. All you had to do was report to them that the gold wasn't there, and then they probably would have given you the real letter."

"Get him out of here!" he shouted at the sergeant.

"Let's go, friend," the sergeant said.

"I'm coming," I told him, but instead I walked up to Martel's desk, picked up the drink he had poured for me and tossed it off.

"Get out!" Martel yelled, his face turning red while he waved his saber around. He couldn't kill me, though, not until he made up his mind whether or not I was right.

I walked to the open door and then turned around with the sergeant's hand on my arm and said to the "general," "Could you tell your cook to cut down on the salt a bit? Thanks."

47

It could have been a few hours or a few days later when they came to take me to see Martel again. He looked much the way he had looked the last time I'd seen him, except that he wasn't waving that saber around, and his face wasn't as red.

"Have a seat, Adams," he said in a subdued tone.

"Thanks."

"Sergeant, get Mr. Adams a drink of whiskey," he told the sergeant.

"Sir?"

"A glass of whiskey, you dolt!" Martel repeated.

"Yes, sir."

The sergeant went over to the table, poured out a glass of whiskey and carried it over to me with a puzzled look on his homely face. I took it and grinned at him.

"That will be all," Martel said then. "Wait outside until I call you."

"Yes, sir."

I sat and nursed my drink, because I didn't know when I'd get another. It all depended on how Martel had decided to play it. I didn't want to rush.

"I've decided that you may be right, Adams," Martel finally said.

"Is that so?"

"Yes."

"That's very generous of you."

"Ah, but you have yet to see the extent of my generosity," he assured me. "It is in light of the fact that we were both seemingly used by the Secret Service that I am offering you the chance to join us."

"What makes you think I would want to join you?" I asked.

"Your government has used you," he said, "played you for a fool. What loyalty do you owe them?"

"You may have a point," I conceded.

"Of course I do, man, of course I do," he said. Now he rose and went to get himself a glass of brandy. At the same time, he brought me the whiskey bottle. Walking back to his desk he said, "You and I would make a fine team. I would make you an officer in my army."

"That is very generous of you," I said. "But I don't know if I want to be an officer in any army that has a Captain Revere." I jerked my thumb towards the outer office for good measure.

"Yes, that is getting to be a problem," Martel said. "The men are starting to resent him."

"I wonder why."

"Perhaps I have chosen the wrong way in which to reward his loyalty."

"Loyalty?" I said. "The only person that rodent is loyal to is himself."

"I think I can guarantee that you won't have any dealings with Revere," he said. "Consider my offer."

"I will," I said, because those two little words would probably keep me alive a little longer.

"Sergeant!"

The door opened and in a moment the sergeant was standing there next to me.

"Sir?"

"Take Mr. Adams to his new quarters. Provided him with bathing facilities and a good meal."

"Sir?"

"Sergeant, just do as you're told," Martel said.

"Yes, sir," the sergeant said. "Come on," he said to me, looking totally bewildered.

"Do you mind?" I asked Martel, holding the bottle up.

"No, of course not. Take it with you."

"Thanks."

I started for the door with the sergeant, then I turned and said, "General?"

"Yes?"

"Why the change of attitude?" I asked. "I mean, what makes you think you'd be any better off with me?"

Martel stood up and walked around the desk to face me. "I know who you are, Adams," he said. "I've known from the beginning. I don't think that having a legend fight for our cause will hurt us one bit, do you?"

"I wouldn't say I was a legend," I said.

"Don't argue with your commanding officer, Adams," Martel said.

"That remains to be seen," I reminded him.

"Go and think it over," he said. "I'm sure you'll agree it's the only thing to do."

Sure, I thought, *since the other choice is death.*

48

"That's just what I need," the sergeant said as he walked me to my new quarters. "First that little jerk Revere, and now you. With my luck, he'll probably make you a colonel."

"If he does that," I told him, "the first thing I'll do is have Revere shot."

He stopped at that, turned and looked at me.

"You might not be so bad after all," he said, and then we walked the rest of the way in silence.

He showed me my new room—which could have looked just like the old one, but well lighted—then showed me where I could take a bath.

"Do you have any clothes for me?" I asked.

"The only clothes we have around here are these uniforms," he said.

I looked at him critically for a few moments, then said, "Maybe you could get me a pair of pants."

"If you throw in with the general, you'll get a whole uniform," he reminded me.

"I haven't decided about that yet," I said.

"You take my advice and tell him anything he wants to hear," the sergeant said. "The man's crazy, and he'll probably kill you if you don't."

"If he's crazy, why are you here?" I asked him.

"I never agreed with Lee," he said, shrugging. "Since the end of the war my life has been a big nothing, then the general came along and I joined up and became somebody again."

"Do you think his New South has a chance?"

He shrugged again and said, "I don't know. That man just might be crazy enough to pull it off. Listen, I'll see if I can rustle you up a pair of pants."

"Okay, thanks."

As he started for the door I called out to him.

"Sarge?"

"Yeah?"

"My horse," I said. "What happened to my horse."

"That big black?" he said, with a look of admiration on his face. "He's fine. That animal is the only horse I've ever seen that looks better than the general's. I heard your horse beat his in a race."

"That's right."

He shook his head and said, "That's some animal you got there, mister."

"Thanks."

"Be a shame for you to die and leave him to one of these morons," he said, and backed out, shutting the door behind him.

I walked to the window and watched him walk across the compound—a man who was only alive during a war, any kind of war.

I went out into the hall and walked down to the bath. There was some clean water there that was lukewarm, which was okay with me. I got in and scrubbed off a couple of inches of dirt and sweat, then walked back down to my new room with a towel around my waist, carrying my clothes and boots in my hands. When I entered the room I saw that the sergeant had been true to his word. He had not only come up with a pair of pants, but with a fairly clean shirt, too. I dropped my pants and shirt into a corner, got into the new ones, then pulled on the same socks and my boots. I felt reasonably better. All I needed now was that meal.

And a gun.

And a way out.

49

The sergeant came back for me and took me to have my good meal, which consisted of steak, beans, bread and coffee. After I'd put that away, I felt better than I had in days.

The room we were in had eight tables, with long benches on each side. I figured you could seat at least eighty men in there at one time.

The sergeant was sitting across from me the whole time, and I was about to ask him a question when Michelle Bouchet Martel walked in. I felt my stomach lurch.

"What's the matter?" he asked me, then he turned and looked at the doorway, where Michelle was standing, staring at me.

"Yeah," he said, turning back. "I know what you mean. She can make a man stop breathing, can't she?"

"Sarge, listen," I said. "I've got to talk to her. You can fix it."

"What? he asked, looking at me like I was crazy. "That's the general's wife, man!"

"I know that," I said. "Look, just get up and go inside, keep the cook busy. Come back in five minutes. That's all I want, Sarge, five minutes."

"Jesus, man, you don't want much," he said.

"Look, I'll pay you," I told him.

"With what?" he asked, laughing.

"You said it yourself," I said. "If I throw in with the general, he'll probably make me a colonel. What's a colonel's pay in the New Confederate Army?"

Now he laughed louder and said, "Same as mine . . . nothing!"

"Nothing?"

"We ain't been paid anything but promises since we started this business," he said, "and I don't mind saying I'm getting tired of it."

He stood up and gave me a stern look.

"I've got to talk to the cook," he said. "Don't go wandering off anywhere without me—you're liable to get yourself shot."

"Yes, sir," I said.

He got up and walked into the kitchen without looking back.

I looked at Michelle and she seemed undecided about whether to come over to the table, but she finally made her decision and walked over.

"Sit down, Michelle," I invited. "We haven't talked in quite a while."

After glancing around worriedly, she sat down opposite me and said, "You have to let me explain, Clint."

"Sure, go ahead," I told her. "We've got about four minutes left."

"I won't try to explain my marriage to Paul . . . . I was on that riverboat because he had gotten word that you would be on that boat."

"What were you supposed to do?" I said. "Get the letter from the messenger?"

"Yes, I was," she confessed. "But what happened between us frightened me so much that I had to leave the boat."

"How?"

"Paul had arranged for a smaller boat to follow us, and pick me up when I signaled."

"How did you explain not getting the letter?"

"I told him I couldn't find the man who had it," she said. "Clint, I didn't know you were the man. I just . . . liked you, and then things got out of hand. I had to leave."

"You could have told me, Michelle."

"No," she said, looking away. "I had to leave while you were asleep, or I . . . I might not have wanted to leave. I paid Henri, the porter, to mislead you about me. He was very gallant, thinking he was helping me avoid a terrible scandal. . . ."

"We can talk all about this when we get out of here," I told her. "Do you want to get out?"

"Oh, yes," she cried, and then looked around to see if anyone heard. Satisfied that no one had, she said, "Paul has gone mad, Clint. He's not the same man I married."

"What about Andy?" I said. "Will she leave?"

She shook her head and said, "Never, but she's hoping I will so she can have Paul."

"How do you feel about that?" I asked.

"They can have each other," she said sadly. "Andrea and I were never really sisters, not the way sisters are supposed to be. I want to get out, Clint."

"All right," I said. "We'll get out."

"How?" she asked.

"Do you have freedom of movement?" I asked.

"Yes."

"You'll have to get me—" I began, but stopped when I saw the sergeant about to come back. "I'll need a gun!" I said quickly.

She surreptitiously handed me a small derringer, then she stood up, threw me a hopeful glance, and hurried from the room.

The derringer had to be Andy's. I wondered what she would do when she found it missing. I was going to have to make my move before then, and there was no time like the present.

I tucked the derringer into my belt as the sergeant came back to the table.

"Still here, huh?" he asked, with a sly smile.

"Where would I go without you, Sarge?" I asked.

"You finished eating?" he asked.

"Yep, all done."

"Come on, I'll take you back to your quarters," he said.

I stood up and said, "No, take me to see the general."

"What for?"

"I've made my decision, and I want to give him my answer," I told him.

"Have you thought this over carefully?" he asked.

"Yep," I said. "I can only see one way out for me, Sarge."

"I guess you've made up your mind, then," the sergeant said. "Come on, I'll take you on over. I hope you made the right decision."

"Sarge," I said, putting my hand over the derringer in my belt, "I've made the only decision."

50

"Wait outside, Sergeant," Martel told the sergeant, and the homely man backed out and shut the door. "Well, I knew all it would take was some cleaning up and a good meal to make you come to your senses," Martel said to me. He came around his desk and put his hand out for me to shake.

"Welcome to the New Confederate Army, Major Adams."

Instead of putting my hand out to him, I took the derringer from my belt and pointed it at his face.

"What's this?"

"It looks tiny," I said, "but it'll still put a hole between your eyes, General. Put that hand over your head, and then hoist the other one right next to it."

"You're mad, Adams," he said, obeying. "You can't get away with this."

"Where's my gun?" I asked him.

"Don't be a fool," he said.

I put the derringer against his temple and said, "I want my gun, General. I'm going to look in your desk, and if it isn't there I'm going to kill you."

"You won't kill me," he said. "I'm your ticket out of here."

"You said it yourself, Martel. I'm mad, remember?" I pressed the barrel of the little gun harder against his head to bring my point home. "Now, turn around with me so I can check your desk."

We turned together, and he was beginning to sweat.

"Don't move," I said, and started backing towards his desk.

"It's not in the desk," he finally said, the words coming out in a rush. "It's in the table where the liquor is."

I kept him covered with the derringer and walked over to the table. There was a small door in the side and when I opened it up I found my gun, and his. I took out mine, strapped it on, then put the derringer away inside my belt. He started to lower his hands and I said, "How would you like seeing how fast I can draw my gun to be the last thing you ever see?"

His eyes widened and he put his hands back up.

"I want you to open that door about a foot and tell the sergeant to bring my horse around, and two others."

"Two others?" he asked. "Who are they for?"

"You'll see," I promised. "Now do as I say, and if you say or do something else, I'll kill you."

He hesitated, then moved to the door and lowered one hand so he could open it.

"Sergeant," he said when he had it open. "Bring around Mr. Adams's horse, and two others."

I heard the sergeant say something and then Martel snapped, "Any two, you idiot!" and shut the door.

"That's good," I said. "Now we'll just relax until the horses are brought around, then you and me are going for a ride."

He turned around and said, "My men will follow, Adams. You'll never get away with it."

"That remains to be seen," I said. I looked at the decanter and then said, "Would you like a brandy—or something stronger?"

"Go to hell," he said, with feeling. "I offer you a chance to join me, share in my dream, and you stab me in the back."

I stared at him for a few moments, and then said, "You blew up your own house, didn't you?"

"Yes, of course," he said. "It was small price to pay, but I had to convince the messenger that I was on the government's side."

"Well, you did that, all right. For a while," I admitted. "But then I began to get suspicious, and maybe that was why you wanted to get rid of me. Tell me, who was it that kept you from killing me, back there on the trail?"

"After Jim Beam struck you—"

"Then you did buy him, didn't you?" I said.

"Oh, yes," he said, smiling, "with promises of gold."

"When?"

"During the journey. I knew you'd be watching me and Revere, so I had him strike you down."

"And why didn't you kill me?"

"Because I love my wife," he said, "and she did not want you killed."

"I see. Then you killed Beam."

"When he was no longer needed, yes," Martel said. "He would not have been true to the cause. He was too greedy."

"I see. And Michelle, will she be true to the cause? And Andy?"

"Michelle is my wife," he said stiffly. "Andrea is her sister. They will be by my side."

He was half right, anyway.

There was a knock on the door, and he looked at me to see what I wanted him to do.

"Just call out," I instructed him.

"What is it?"

"The horses are ready, sir." It was the sergeant's voice. "They're out front."

I nodded and Martel said, "Very well."

"All right," I said. "Let's go out." I drew my gun and said, "If anyone makes a move towards me, you're a dead man."

"I would gladly give my life for my cause," he said.

"Martel, if you die," I said, "so does the cause. These men will scatter without your leadership."

He nodded shortly and said, "You're right, Adams. I'll do as you say, but I'll come after you."

"Fine. Let's go."

He walked to the door ahead of me and opened it. Outside, Revere and the sergeant both looked up.

"Sir—" Revere began, but Martel made a chopping motion with his hand, silencing him.

"What's going on?" the sergeant said.

"I'm leaving, Sarge," I said. "And I'm taking the general with me. If anybody makes a wrong move, I'll kill him. Go outside and tell everyone that."

The sergeant looked from me to his commanding officer, and Martel said, "Do as he says."

"Yes, sir," the sergeant said, and he went outside.

"You can't do this," Joey Revere said.

"Come here, Revere," I said. I don't think I'd ever disliked a man more—a man who had never actually done me any harm.

"*Captain* Revere," he said, smirking.

I pointed my gun at him and cocked it for effect.

"Come here," I repeated.

The skirm on his face was replaced by a doubtful look, but he came around his desk and walked over to me.

"W-what are you going to do?" he stammered.

"Just satisfy an urge," I said. I swung my gun and laid it against the side of his head, knocking him over backwards. He fell to the floor and lay there, unconscious.

"I must admit," Martel said, "I've wanted to do that myself, on occasion."

"Let's go outside," I told him.

He walked ahead of me and opened the door. As we stepped out I saw Duke, the palomino, and two other horses.

"Somebody can't count," I told Martel. "You've got a good group of men here, General."

His men were all standing around, watching, and some of them looked nervous. Some of them looked as if they didn't care what happened, one way or the other.

"You better hope none of them gets too nervous," I said to him.

"Don't anyone touch their gun," he called. "I'm riding out with this man, but I'll be back."

Off to one side I saw Michelle and Andy, both looking sad and worried, but for different reasons.

"Michelle," I called out, "mount up. We're leaving."

She hesitated, then turned to Andy and said something. Her younger sister refused to look at her and shook her head. Michelle came forward and started to mount one of the horses.

"Get on the palomino," I told her, and she obeyed.

"Okay, General, it's your turn. Climb aboard."

We moved forward and he mounted one of the other horses. I looked at the faces of the men around us, then I walked to Duke and started to mount up.

There was a shot behind me, and I turned with my gun ready. One of the soldiers was on the ground, clutching at his chest, and his gun was in the dirt.

I looked around to see who had shot him, and saw the sergeant standing there with his gun in his hand. He holstered his gun and gave me a small salute. I smiled, turned, and mounted Duke.

"Who's the fourth horse for?" Michelle asked.

"Somebody who decided to stay after all," I told her. I don't think the sergeant expected Martel to return. He probably expected to become even more of a somebody when the "General" was gone. The fourth horse had been his out, just in case he changed his mind at the last minute.

As Michelle, Martel, and I rode out through the front gates of the small, once-abandoned fort, I silently wished him luck.

EPILOGUE

When we finally came within sight of a town large enough to have a telegraph office, I turned to Martel and said, "Okay, General, this is as far as you go."

"What do you mean?" he demanded.

"Oh, I'm not going to kill you," I said, "if that's what you're worried about."

"You're not going to take me to Washington and turn me in?" he asked.

I shook my head.

"I'm not going back to Washington," I said. "I'm heading for Texas." That was where I'd left my rig, and that was the only place I wanted to go.

"What about your job?" he asked.

"My job was to deliver to you a totally useless letter, which I did. It's over. You can go back to the fort, or wherever you want to go."

"You *are* mad," he said. "I'll go back to the fort, gather my men and the New South will rise."

"General," I said, shifting in my saddle. "You haven't got any gold; by the time you get back to the fort half of what men you had will be following a new leader; and when I get into that town, I'll telegraph all the information I have about you to

Washington. They'll have a platoon of soldiers out to your fort so fast, your head will spin. The New South has fallen before it even had a chance to rise."

I turned to Michelle and said, "You're free to go where you want, now."

Martel said to her, "Michelle—"

"I can't go with you, Paul," she said. Then she looked at me and said, "And I can't go with you, either."

"Come to town with me," I said. "I'm sure you'll be able to find a stage to somewhere. Or maybe we can . . . talk."

She looked at me, then at Paul Martel again, and then she moved her head towards me again and nodded.

"Michelle—"

"You better get going, General," I said.

He gave me a puzzled, helpless look and said, "But . . . where?"

"Hey, that's up to you," I said. "You're the general. Make a decision."

I started riding, and Michelle rode alongside me. Neither one of us looked back.

I sent my message to Washington, with a few choice words added for Fenton and Ulysses S. Grant. Words that I wouldn't trust myself to deliver in person. Martel had been right about one thing. I had been used, and I didn't like it, but what could I do about it? Could I fight the government? Wasn't that what Martel had planned to do?

No, I couldn't fight them, but I damn well didn't have to go back to Washington and be in the same room with them. Not after the way they'd used me.

Hell of a way to treat a legend.

J. R. ROBERTS
THE GUNSMITH
SERIES

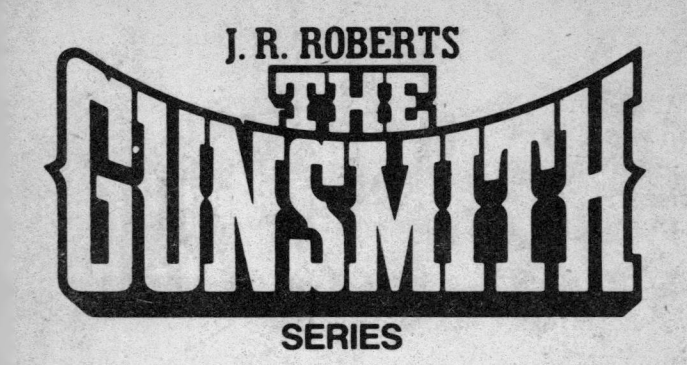

☐ 30928-3	THE GUNSMITH	#1:	MACKLIN'S WOMEN	$2.50
☐ 30857-0	THE GUNSMITH	#2:	THE CHINESE GUNMEN	$2.25
☐ 30858-9	THE GUNSMITH	#3:	THE WOMAN HUNT	$2.25
☐ 30859-7	THE GUNSMITH	#4:	THE GUNS OF ABILENE	$2.25
☐ 30925-9	THE GUNSMITH	#5:	THREE GUNS FOR GLORY	$2.50
☐ 30861-9	THE GUNSMITH	#6:	LEADTOWN	$2.25
☐ 30862-7	THE GUNSMITH	#7:	THE LONGHORN WAR	$2.25
☐ 30901-1	THE GUNSMITH	#8:	QUANAH'S REVENGE	$2.50
☐ 30864-3	THE GUNSMITH	#9:	HEAVYWEIGHT GUN	$2.25
☐ 30924-0	THE GUNSMITH	#10:	NEW ORLEANS FIRE	$2.50
☐ 30866-X	THE GUNSMITH	#11:	ONE-HANDED GUN	$2.25
☐ 30926-7	THE GUNSMITH	#12:	THE CANADIAN PAYROLL	$2.50

Available at your local bookstore or return this form to:

C CHARTER BOOKS
Book Mailing Service
P.O. Box 690, Rockville Centre, NY 11571

Please send me the titles checked above. I enclose _____. Include 75¢ for postage and handling if one book is ordered; 25¢ per book for two or more not to exceed $1.75. California, Illinois, New York and Tennessee residents please add sales tax.

NAME _____

ADDRESS _____

CITY _____ STATE/ZIP _____

(allow six weeks for delivery.)   A1/a

J.R. ROBERTS
THE GUNSMITH
SERIES

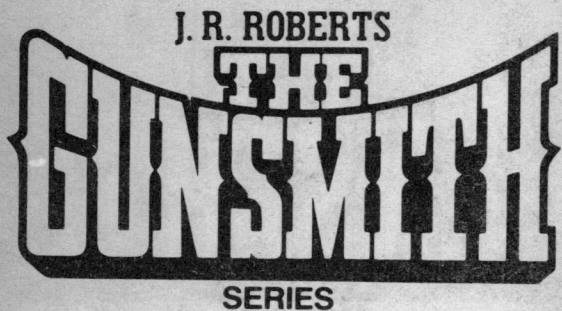

☐ 30927-5	THE GUNSMITH #13: DRAW TO AN INSIDE DEATH	$2.50
☐ 30922-4	THE GUNSMITH #14: DEAD MAN'S HAND	$2.50
☐ 30872-4	THE GUNSMITH #15: BANDIT GOLD	$2.25
☐ 30886-4	THE GUNSMITH #16: BUCKSKINS AND SIX-GUNS	$2.25
☐ 30887-2	THE GUNSMITH #17: SILVER WAR	$2.25
☐ 30889-9	THE GUNSMITH #18: HIGH NOON AT LANCASTER	$2.25
☐ 30890-2	THE GUNSMITH #19: BANDIDO BLOOD	$2.25
☐ 30891-0	THE GUNSMITH #20: THE DODGE CITY GANG	$2.25
☐ 30892-9	THE GUNSMITH #21: SASQUATCH HUNT	$2.25
☐ 30893-7	THE GUNSMITH #22: BULLETS AND BALLOTS	$2.25
☐ 30894-5	THE GUNSMITH #23: THE RIVERBOAT GANG	$2.25

Available at your local bookstore or return this form to:

CHARTER BOOKS
Book Mailing Service
P.O. Box 690, Rockville Centre, NY 11571

Please send me the titles checked above. I enclose _____. Include 75¢ for postage and handling if one book is ordered; 25¢ per book for two or more not to exceed $1.75. California, Illinois, New York and Tennessee residents please add sales tax.

NAME_____

ADDRESS_____

CITY_____ STATE/ZIP_____

(allow six weeks for delivery.)

A1